only

ever

always

only ever always

Penni Russon

Delacorte Press

 Published in the United States by Delacorte Press, an imprint of Random House Children's Books, a division of Random House, Inc., New York. Originally published in slightly different form in Australia by Allen & Unwin, Sydney, in 2011.

Delacorte Press is a registered trademark and the colophon is a trademark of Random House, Inc.

Visit us on the Web! randomhouse.com/teens

Educators and librarians, for a variety of teaching tools, visit us at RHTeachersLibrarians.com

Library of Congress Cataloging-in-Publication Data
Russon, Penni.
Only ever always / Penni Russon. —1st American ed.
p. cm.
Summary: The notes of an old music box connects two girls from very different worlds—Clara, who struggles to survive poverty and violence in a troubled city, and Claire, whose ordinary life is beset by grief—in a place where neither can be sure what is real.
ISBN 978-0-385-74352-5 (hc : alk. paper)—ISBN 978-0-449-81668-4 (ebook)—
ISBN 978-0-375-99119-6 (glb : alk. paper)
[1. Music box—Fiction. 2. Supernatural—Fiction. 3. Space and time—Fiction.
4. Dogs—Fiction.] I. Title.
PZ7.R91940n1 2013
[Fic]—dc23
2012025063

The text of this book is set in 12-point Granjon.
Book design by Trish Parcell

Printed in the United States of America

10 9 8 7 6 5 4 3 2 1

First American Edition

For Zoë—only ever always

DOUBTS

When she sleeps, her soul, I know,
Goes a wanderer on the air,
Wings where I may never go,
Leaves her lying, still and fair,
Waiting, empty, laid aside,
Like a dress upon a chair . . .
This I know, and yet I know
Doubts that will not be denied.

For if the soul be not in place,
What has laid trouble in her face?
And, sits there nothing ware and wise
Behind the curtains of her eyes,
What is it, in the self's eclipse,
Shadows, soft and passingly,
About the corners of her lips,
The smile that is essential she?

And if the spirit be not there,
Why is fragrance in the hair?

—Rupert Brooke

"I had a dream," Groom tells. "It was you and me. We was travelin to make somethin new. A beginnin." He lays his hand on mine, and I twitch with the warmth of it. "Would you?"

I pull my hand away. "This now?"

"Some day. Some night or other."

"And where would we be going? Where is there to go where there's beginnings?"

Groom's still dreaming, looking past what is, into his imaginings. "In my dream we crossed the river."

Crossing the river is the kind of mad thing Groom would say. Groom, who can't always tell the difference between folly and sense. I think about the dank sickly greenness, the greasy things that hunt in the river's shadow.

"What about dogs? What about trick currents and sink-holes and ending up with a stomach full of mud? Them's the stories what happen when you try and cross the river."

"Them's the stories we know, Clara, ones what tried and couldn't. There's others."

"Who drowned to the bottom," I scoff.

"Or didn't."

"Aint no one who's been across the river returned."

"Maybe they found somethin better."

"What's the point," I say, and I won't look at the sparkling hope in his eyes the same rich murk as the river, "of going nowhere? We aint like Andrew. We aint got an afore. Or an after. This is what we know."

"Andrew," spits Groom. "Across the river might be adventure, across the river might be freedom."

In the deep of me I wouldn't mind an adventure, but I aint laying myself bare to Groom, not when he's in a mood for calling folly sense. And I aint giving myself over to hoping. Hoping is what unstitches you, leaving you open for other things to waft in, like fear. Like hopelessness. "And aint I free?" I grump. "Nobody tells me what to do."

"Funny sort of freedom. You got more Bosses than you can imagine, lordin over us, waitin for us to step out of the shadow so they can make their sport of us, or use us to do their work. All right then. Not for adventure, if you aint got the gut for it. But say you'll come with me anyway. For the dreamin o' it. Just for dreamin."

"Dreams are nothing, not even air. You wake up and pop, like a greasy soap bubble, they're gone. Dreams don't matter none. They don't last."

"Sometimes they matter," tells Groom, but fadingly. He sounds distant, uncertain. "Sometimes they last."

"Claire!" Mum calls from the bottom of the stairs, and the dream dissolves.

You sit up and blink. The dream took you by surprise, clear and resounding as a bell, as though it were waiting for you all along. Littered on your bed are oddments, junk, bric-a-brac, the assorted miscellanea of your life, one-eyed dolls and threadbare teddy bears, two wooden ducks on wheels once joined now split, metal cars, wooden tops. Most of indeterminate value, things without history, but for the fact that they have lived here so long they have become part of you, and you couldn't bear to excise any of them.

You are supposed to be sorting through the cacophony of things that clutter your bedroom, the things you call treasures. (You, who never throw anything away, who have held everything dear that has come into your possession from babyhood.) Tonight Uncle Charlie and his wife, Pia, are coming to dinner. Soon their first baby will be born, and

Mum thinks it would be nice if you pass on some of the toys you've outgrown. But you are not sure it is possible to outgrow the things that have built you from nothing into something. For who are you before you own anything? A naked grub, a nothing.

There is a weight in your arms. You have slept holding the music box to your chest. In fact, it was the rise and fall of the music box tune that made you drift off in the first place. It isn't truly a box, but a glass globe, containing a miniature world, which slowly revolves as the music plays. A few stray notes spring free as you place the music box on your bedside table and for a moment you catch a strong odor wafting out of your dream: a smell of dampness and forgetting.

The music box was your first treasure. Charlie bought it for you when you were just new. You know that there would be a certain poetry in passing it on to his baby, like a family heirloom that may perhaps one day wend its way back to *your* baby. But it is yours, so very yours, a part of the being of you. How can you relinquish it? How can you let any of these precious things go? They are all you.

"Claire!"

You pull yourself off the bed and slump downstairs, your black school shoes resounding on the wooden staircase.

"I thought you were going to change," Mum scolds. "Did you finish sorting through those things?" She frowns clairvoyantly at your bird's-nest hair. "Have you been asleep? Oh, Claire, I hope you weren't wearing your shoes in bed."

You shrug.

"I was just about to head next door. I picked up some pills

for Mrs. Jarvis when I was down the street and I thought maybe you could go instead. They're always asking after you, and now you're in high school you never see them."

"But *Mu-um*—!" The Jarvises are old. Their oldness wafts from them, a stale odor, and clings to everything.

You are formulating an excuse about homework when the phone in the hallway shrilly interrupts. Mum picks it up, holding you in place with a gesture. "Hello?" She frowns. "Hello? Pia, is that you? This is a terrible line, I can hardly hear you." Mum motions to you and thrusts the pills at you, jabbing her finger in the direction of next door.

"Are Pia and Charlie still coming to dinner?" you ask. Your mother shoos you away. You *want* them to come, the days and weeks drag by without them when Pia is away playing piano with orchestras all over the world, and Charlie travels with her. You do love them so. But you are not ready to give up the music box, or any of your things. "Hang up," she is saying. "And I'll call you back. You're *where*?" She covers the mouthpiece and hisses, "Straight there and back, Claire. No hanging around on the street."

Outside the afternoon air is thin with the last of the winter sun. You hesitate at the dividing strip of garden that separates your driveway from the Jarvises'. You glance at the street and see a smudge of yellow, barely painted onto the winter street.

It is a dog, alone and unleashed. You stiffen. You have little experience of dogs except to know they are unpredictable. Especially dogs that look as unloved as this one, with its protruding rib cage and patchy yellow coat, and pale scarred belly.

The dog sees you and barks. You glimpse the slippery gleam of long tooth. You don't have enough of the language of dogs to guess whether it intends friendliness or harm. You breathe for a few beats, eye to eye. Then the dog is gone. Not *vanished,* for you can see it trotting down the street, nose down, sniffing its path. Just gone.

You turn to the Jarvises' door and knock. Yellow bottle glass frames the door, distorting the hallway within. A blurred figure approaches, swimming in the pool of golden light. Young Mrs. Jarvis answers the door. Young Mrs. Jarvis has starchy gray curls that sit up around her face. She wears her usual slightly surprised expression, as if this isn't quite the life she expected having. Young Mrs. Jarvis is only young in comparison to her elderly mother-in-law, who, for as far back as you can remember, has always been impossibly old.

"Oh, hello, Claire!" Instead of taking the proffered pills, she ushers you inside, the very thing you hoped to avoid.

You follow Mrs. Jarvis down the hall, dragging your feet. You are not interested in lingering in the Jarvises' house with its sharp laundered scent that fails to overpower the underlying musty human smell of the aged, unwashed in their creases.

You are led into the small dim wallpapered living room. Old Mrs. Jarvis sits at a tea tray with metal legs. On it is a carefully folded newspaper that she does not appear to be reading and a cup of thin black coffee, daintily set on a saucer. One corner of her mouth droops a little, and so does her left eye. Her hair is sparse and white.

"Look. We have a visitor."

Old Mrs. Jarvis does not move. You fold your hands in front of you and knot your fingers tightly together.

"Cup of tea, dear?" Young Mrs. Jarvis asks. "Kettle's just boiled." She is out of the room before you find your voice to say *no.*

You are frozen, breathing shadows deep into your lungs; all the air in here was used up long ago. You step gingerly forward and place the pills on the tea tray. As you do, a rusted, unpracticed noise emerges from the old woman's throat and you bend closer to make out the words.

"Teatime tattle," the old lady creaks. She looks up at you.

The old lady is so frail a puff of wind could blow her away, yet her gaze is steady and alert. Her hands grip the arms of her chair, and a stream of words pours from her mouth. "Looks genuine improver. Hidden strings. Chance in harder event. Must come into contention. Will appreciate rise in distance."

You step back, almost knocking over a set of nested tables.

Young Mrs. Jarvis appears at the doorway. "Don't mind her. She's bedeviled by those damn racehorses. Now, how do you take your tea?"

"*No,* thank you!" you finally gasp. "My mother's expecting me home."

Even with your back turned, you know the older woman's eyes are still fixed on you. "Go well," rasps Old Mrs. Jarvis as you stumble up the hallway toward the sweet air of release. "Go well." Words which seem intended to comfort but have the exact opposite effect on you. "Go well. Keep safe. Go well."

You burst into the stillness of your own house. The hallway is empty, the phone replaced on its cradle. The kitchen, where you expect to find your mother and the smell of roasting meat perhaps or hear the friendly sizzle of sausages, is cold and vacant, all gleaming surfaces. Finally you discover Mum in the family room, sitting on a chair, staring at the television, which isn't on. Its big blank eye stares back at her.

"Mum?"

Her head turns in the direction of your voice, but she doesn't seem to see you, not right away. Finally her eyes focus on your face.

"Oh, Claire," Mum says, sounding broken and far away. "Oh, Claire."

"What? Is it Dad? Is it Pia? Something's wrong with the baby!"

"No. Not the baby. It's Charlie."

You trail after your mother from room to room as she gathers the things Charlie might need in the hospital. Freshly washed pajamas (Dad's, but they would fit) from the laundry. A cake of Pears soap that smells of the distinctive blend of cola drinks and apples, reminding you in some vague way of Christmases at your grandmother's house near the beach. A toothbrush, still in its packet, from the bathroom cabinet, a towel from the linen cupboard, warm socks from Dad's drawer.

"Can I come?" you ask.

"No, sweetie."

"Please! I want to see Charlie."

"If you were there, I would have to take care of you. And it's Pia who needs me."

"I can look after Pia too. I'm old enough."

"No," Mum says.

"I can comfort you. Charlie's *your* brother."

"He was so little when our mother died, I've always taken responsibility for him. He's more like—" Mum gulps in a mouthful of air. She presses her lips together until they go white. "Claire, I said no. Just leave it at that."

You follow your mother into the master bedroom and perch on the edge of your parents' bed, watching your mother make up her face. You are not allowed to wear makeup, though lots of the girls at school have lip gloss and even eyeliner or glittery stuff for their cheeks.

"You think Charlie drives too fast," you say.

"He does drive too fast. Zipping in and out of lanes."

"You think he's *reckless*."

"He could be safer. He could take precautions; drop back instead of charging ahead." Mum looks at herself in the mirror, dabbing eye shadow aggressively onto her eyelids. There is a connection there, you think hazily. A connection between Charlie driving too fast and the fact that you aren't allowed eye shadow and lipstick, but you are too addled to follow that thought.

Instead you say: "You think it's his fault."

"I don't know, Claire. Pia said he was between two trucks on the freeway and one of them changed lanes without seeing him. He had nowhere to go."

"You say motorbikes are invisible on the road."

Mum turns and looks at you. "Me saying those things didn't make this happen."

"Charlie didn't make it happen either. It was the truck. If anyone's to blame it's the truck driver who didn't look properly. Nothing's *invisible.* Not really. Everything *real* can be seen." And no one is more real than Charlie. He smells of petrol and ink. He has big flat hands, with rough broken skin and thick stubbed nails.

"Charlie's about to be a daddy. He shouldn't be riding motorbikes anymore. He has responsibilities. The world *isn't* safe. He has to learn that. He has to learn to *take care*!"

Suddenly a strange tearing sob comes out of your mother, one and then another. For a moment she can't breathe. You stare at her in horror. When she was all business, easing the toothbrush out of its wrapping, finding a plastic case for the soap, you had been quite sure that this was just an ordinary sort of accident, two broken legs perhaps, even a broken neck. But to see your mother overcome . . . now you are frightened. Now you realize just how serious things are.

You sit, together and apart, on the stairs—Mum on the bottom step, you about halfway up—waiting for Dad. Mum zips and unzips the overnight bag next to her on the step and from behind she looks like a teenager going to school camp.

The back of her neck looks lonely. Perhaps it is the way her head tilts down, and her dark hair falling into her face.

Dad's key scrapes in the lock. He sits on the step next to Mum. They wrap their arms around each other and Mum lets herself be held without saying anything. Longing creeps over you; you also want to be enclosed. At the same time your skin prickles with resistance and you shift one step farther up.

Your parents are fragile. They are as lost as you are in the face of this, and as lonesome. Something cold crawls under your skin. You feel orphaned.

Mum stands to leave.

You stand too.

"Is Charlie going to die?"

A quick silent exchange passes between Mum and Dad.

"No," says Mum. "No. Charlie is not going to die."

"Lydia," Dad murmurs.

"*Promise* me," you beg, though you suspect it's dangerous to ask for such a promise.

"Lydia, you can't," Dad says.

"We have to think positively," Mum says to Dad. "We have to *will it*." She grabs you severely by the wrists. "I promise you." You feel yourself open up, and a hollow wind blows in. "Charlie is not going to die. Everything is going to be *fine*."

The bedclothes retain the wrinkled depression of your body where it lay this afternoon. Littered on the bed are toys, treasures, trinkets. Refuse, rubbish, relics.

You no longer know how to look at these items. All at once they seem more important than ever—the evidence of you, the earthly traces that will outlive you, that will stand in for you when the body of you and with it the spirit or soul or whatever it is that is encased inside has slipped away, as Charlie could slip away.

And yet the one-eyed, loose-wigged dolls, the threadbare teddies, the irreconcilably separated wooden ducks suddenly chill you with their staring lifelessness. These are husks only, empty vessels, your child's imagination has departed them and they no longer live. It is the objects that are dead, horrifyingly empty. You sweep them to the floor in sudden anger, and it is the rage of the child you once were, powerful in your disappointment, filling the room.

You pick up the music box and with blinding white-hot rage you hold it above your head. You imagine it wrecked, the glass globe cracked open, the world inside dashed to pieces. The picture of it gives you a ghastly satisfaction. But rushing up to meet this appetite for destruction is grief and shame. Grief tempers rage and all you are left with is hollow shame.

And you are sorry. You gently place the music box on your bedside table with trembling hands. You pick up the closest doll—Martha—and smooth the cotton cap her hair is woven into back over her exposed, plastic, glue-stained scalp. You place her carefully on a shelf. You do the same for the next doll and the poor brown teddy who landed facedown, the metal cars, the family of felt-eared bunnies. You lean the wooden ducks against each other, carefully balancing them so the cracks don't show.

The street outside is quiet.

A moth taps lightly against the window. You watch it, imagining its flight path through the city as a dotted line, a glistening thread trailing through the darkness—looping, spooling, entangling space, from one house to the next, around letterboxes, over the road, spinning through the air. And now here it is, stuttering against the glass, romancing the warm light inside. The yellow light remains perfectly indifferent. From far above its twin—the moon—looks on. As you watch the moth, a feeling bubbles up from a deep forgotten past, an ancient self, someone you were before you were Claire: a memory is triggered but instantly forgotten again. It is a feeling from a dream, breathless and fizzing, and with it comes a familiar sense of music about to begin, as though, if you concentrate hard enough, you could snatch the passing notes out of the air.

"Not asleep yet?" Dad asks from the door.

"Has Mum called?"

Dad shakes his head.

"I can't sleep," you say, though you haven't tried.

Dad picks up the music box from the bedside table, where you placed it earlier. You are struck by an image you never saw, or that you witnessed but couldn't retain except as a story you have been told over and over since before you can remember, an image of Charlie bringing this box to the hospital when you were only a few hours old, arriving with it under his arm, in a rush of outside air and panic and love.

Dad winds the box and places it down beside you. He lifts the covers of your bed, and you shimmy down under the blankets. The music is so familiar that you remember the notes as much as hear them. It is not just the music you hear, it is also the mechanism, the faint metallic grind. You close your eyes and the music soaks into your skin. As the music box winds down, the spaces between the notes grow longer, and your heart aches, waiting for each note to fall. Finally you can't bear it. You sit up and wind the box again, and the music cascades once more in a silvery rush.

This time you roll over on your side to watch. Inside the globe dance a girl and her partner, a mouse in top hat and tails. The girl and the mouse spin together, circling the interior of their enclosed world. At their feet grow flowers, bespeckled by tiny insects, and if you shake their world, more flowers rain down on the mouse and his bride. In the back of the globe there is a piece of stiff card, a little faded now, with an intricately painted setting that looks like a wedding: a feast laid on a long table surrounded by a small party of guests watching the solemn mouse and the laughing, twirling girl.

As a child you were fascinated with the miniature, wishing you were small enough to drink from an acorn cup or to sleep suspended in a moss bird's nest. You watched this very scene on countless nights before you drifted off to sleep, wishing you could enter their world in your dreams, taking your place in the painted background among the gentlemanly hedgehogs and the frocked bunnies, the molded jellies and layered cakes. But try as you might, you cannot make your own dreams.

"Will you draw on my back?" you ask your father. He sits down next to you and his finger swirls across your back, the way he used to when you were small, making rivers and mountains and oceans, crisscrossing latitudes and longitudes. But before you are quite asleep, he stands up and walks over to the window. You watch him through half-open eyes. He looks out, over the darkening rooftop of the house next door, to the next rooftop and the next, all tight lids on other people's lives.

And you wonder. Is loving someone too big a risk? Is it better to seal yourself up, to not let love in or out? Mum is careful who she loves. This is why you have little experience of dogs. She has never let you have a pet, you are sure, in order to set an example about loving sparingly. If Charlie is lost, is everyone who loves Charlie lost too? How will you face Pia? How will you be able to bear her sadness? How will she bear yours?

Dad sighs and pulls the curtain sharply closed.

Outside, the moth—its enchantment broken—spirals upward, away into the night. Rising, spinning, a hopeless tattered thing, of dust. You rise with it, into the night sky. The night is tense with musical possibility, as if, between the notes from the music box that you can still hear ascending, there is the shadow of other notes, a song not yet sung. A song from a dream perhaps. And here in the half-light between waking and sleep, you remember that this afternoon, before the Jarvises, before Charlie, you *were* dreaming, a faraway dream about a faraway girl, a girl who looked just like you but was living another life. The music carries you. You rise. You rise up. And, spread out among the frozen stars, finally, you sleep. . . .

What have I got?

This city's crumbling to nothing, to rubble round me. I walk and walk and scour and sift and quarry. I find what's left. Crumbles what might mean something to someone. Crumbles of plastic or painted wood, sometimes with glass eyes or yellow hair, or some have wheels or buttons or strings. Crumbles with moving parts, what once used to make their own sounds or flash their spinning lights, but now just sit there and say nothing. Like me, Andrew tells. Some days I don't say nothing to no one, but my hair aint yellow, it's brown as dust. Some days all Andrew does is talk and talk, talking about what used to be afore, but I don't remember afore. Far as I know there's only been this, nothing piled on nothing, there's only been crumbles and quarrying. I don't remember things whole. Everything's always been broke.

Andrew tells that once I would have had a mother and a

father, right back when I was begun, but I don't remember that neither. He said they might have been whole or they might have been broke but that's not what matters. What matters, Andrew tells, is that they was mine, they joined themselves up together and started me. By the time Andrew came along I didn't have them anymore, I was a thing alone, and, he tells, I didn't speak for days. I was quiet as a bug and as low to the ground. I scuttled, and he makes me laugh doing it, scrabbling on his hands and feet till he collapses. He thought I couldn't walk up on my two feet, but he was wrong. He thought I couldn't talk neither, but then one night he woke up to find me standing by the bed, wide-eyed, with a jumbling of words coming out of my mouth. Real words, but not put together in any way that made sense. Just words they were. Carrot and moon and dirt and picture and dog dog dog. He thought I might be broke too, somewhere inside me, but I weren't, I was just dreaming, and after that night, he tells, I spoke proper to him, like all I needed was my springs loosened—I seen that with the crumbles.

Andrew tells this. He found me and the house at the same time and liked us enough to stay. But even being found was afore my memory began. I don't know what I remember first. Just this I suppose. The empty broke-down houses, the rummaging, market, Andrew, his Doctor. Nothing much changes, 'cept some of the faces at market and that every year I get a bit taller. Not Andrew, though, he's done with his growing and it aint done him any good but got his head closer to the ceiling and one day that's gonna fall in on us. He reckons if I listen to him I ought to stop with it too, but there's not much I can do about growing, though being grown don't interest me none. Besides, it aint like I'm ever gonna be real tall like Andrew, I'm slowed down already and I aint even up to his armpits.

Anyway, as usual the day ends and I head for home with my haul. Some tins without wrappers, but heavy with food still inside, some broken bits—aint none of 'em good, but maybe I can make something of 'em—this one's got wheels, this one's got some kind of motor and one's got one real good eye. No batteries tonight. Batteries is best for swapping. I don't find batteries much anymore. Some say things are getting harder. But they was always hard. I got one more thing too, tucked real careful under my arm and I'm twittering inside, I can't wait to give it to Andrew. It aint worth much to nobody but us, but I look after it real careful just the same.

Our house aint got no front. It's just rooms bared to the world, and a big staircase going up. You can see right inside it from the street, upstairs and down. Inside the rooms is piles of rubble, broken pieces of front and ceiling and glass; the inside walls coming down in pieces and broken bits of furniture and just-picked-through junk. Everything good is gone. The dogs have done a job on it, they've marked it all over and it stinks. Dogs live there for times, then they move on. There's more dogs than people in the city, that's facts. Andrew's been out of the city, that's where he come from, where there's more people than dogs, and he says that's worse.

Me and Andrew live in two rooms at the back. It was a big house afore it got broke and there were lots of rooms. Our two rooms are still pretty good, the back of the house is stuck on tight. There's a room upstairs too that is still whole, though all closed up, windows blacked. We can't get into it through the rubble in the front or climbing from outside—like we haven't tried enough times!—so it just sits up there, closed and quiet, thinking its own thoughts, hoarding secrets and ghosts and insect shells and crumbles and bones. There could be batteries or anything up there, but I can't see in. Andrew won't force it. He's feared that if we start banging things round, maybe the house will fall in, and probably that room is full of nothing but stale air. We like it here, Andrew and me, enough to leave that room be, but he can't stop me thinking about it, and in my mind there's more up there than old empty air.

"Andrew!" I call out as I round the back of the house. But I know he aint home yet. I hate that Doctor. He wants Andrew to go and live with him all the time, he don't care nothing about me. But we can't count both our fortunes on the street and that's why Andrew goes there. Doctor gives him things we need, like fruit and veg and candles and matches and stuff. Bits here and bits there, but sometimes Andrew comes home with a real haul. He calls it Christmas. I don't know what that means, but that's how he calls it: "Christmas is here."

I leave the crumbles outside, Andrew don't like them in the house, especially the ones what have eyes. He minds that there's enough rubbish out there without bringing it in with us. I take the tins in though and pile them in with the others. I put the other thing on the table so Andrew will see it first when he gets home, he won't mind that. I stroke it down flat, there's a few little folds and wrinkles, but apart from that it's real fine. Hopefully there'll be light enough for it when Andrew gets home.

I open a tin. It's fruit. The juice is thick sweet and trickles down my throat and sloshes up into the back of my nose.

By the time Andrew gets home it's dark outside. He picks up the treasure and turns it over, a faint smile on his lips. Candlelight jumps and twitches.

"Have we had it afore?" I ask.

Andrew shakes his head. I can see that he's tired, more tired than usual tonight. He's quiet. Andrew's not regularly quiet.

"Good," I say.

Andrew puts the thing down. "Not tonight, Clara," he tells, though I aint asked yet.

I don't say nothing. But I kick the leg of his chair. I open him a tin. More fruit. But he puts his head down at the table and starts to snore, right there, still sitting, like some of them leftovers you see in the houses, what aint got skin no more.

I kick his chair again, but he don't wake. I kick his leg, hard enough to bruise. I bang the tins round. I slurp his fruit. He don't stir. It's lonely being awake by myself. But I don't want to sleep. Sleeping is lonely too. The house creaks. Dogs call to each other in the falling night.

For company, I take the treasure off the table, where Andrew left it, and I smooth back the first page. I sound out the flickering words and though I know the letters, I can't always tell what they mean all put together.

"Once," I say out loud, my finger dragging my eyes across the page. Something moves in the stalks outside, weeds rustle their tips together. "Upon a." Somewhere in the broke-down city a dog barks. "Time."

To get to market I used to walk by the river and through the park, but Groom tells there's dogs now. River dogs are wild, wilder than street dogs, they're solitary and sulfur-breathed, eyes flicker through the trees, they watch. I say I aint feared of dogs. But Groom and Andrew make me promise to walk streetways when I'm alone. There's dogs on streets too I sniff, but I give Groom a hair when I promise and he wraps it round his finger. Andrew don't need a hair, just words is enough for him, cause he's got a look and can see when I'm making lies.

Andrew tells that river and city used to be all the same, one running through and the other growing round. But not no more. River is a dark territory, it keeps the city apart, it makes two cities. City crumbles. River grows.

Market runs day and into night, people come, people go, sometimes there's plenty, sometimes not. I never been at night, but Groom has. Groom lives on the edge of the park, in the Zone. He makes pleadings that I should live there too, safety in numbers, he tells. But me and Andrew got a number already, even if it is only two. That's what works and I know you don't fix nothing that aint broke.

But I'd like to see a night market. They're different, Groom tells, but when I ask different how his mouth closes tight and he don't tell. *Jus' different.* Different good or different bad? His mouth's so tight his seams are fit to bursting, like an overstuffed crumble. *Jus' different.*

Andrew is feared that I got an adventuring spirit, and he don't. But I love Andrew and I would never go adventuring without him, even if sometimes I look after Groom with moons in my eyes, wishing for something I don't have.

My bag's knobbly, filled with insides, and it bangs my legs till I feel bruised all over. Metal things: magnets, springs, cogs and wheels. There's ones what will use 'em, ones what make, ones what fix, ones what like to spring-load their traps. And you can use the bolt ends to shoot dogs. Andrew don't let me make nothing like that. *Clara, knowing you you'll shoot your own ear right off and trap your thumbs for measure,* he tells. Don't mean I aint tried. But I trapped something once that weren't my thumb, a small thing, gray and greasy, and it lay there staring and pulsing and I didn't like it, the way it looked at me and then died. So I buried it under stones, trap and all, I kicked it there then buried it. I didn't want to touch it. But burying it didn't forget it. I could still see it dying, its glass eyes open, like windows of a house left open with no one, nothing, no walls inside.

I turn up the main street. The sun is a white hole in the white sky. Down the ends of the streets that come off the main road I see flashes of river. I hear a distant dog's bark. From the river's glooming another calls back.

I walk past the big houses. Round here's where Andrew's Doctor lives. The houses aint whole, but Andrew tells that sometimes there's one perfect room with carpet and trickly glass things that hang down from the ceiling and colored paper on the walls and that's where they live—the folk like Andrew's Doctor who live better than what we do, though

I don't see how things can be that much better in one place than another.

You don't see much people on the streets. When Andrew was a kid everyone went out in the morning at the same time. I seen cars afore, but Andrew tells the roads were full of 'em all at once driving and bipping. I can't imagine that. Now you don't see much people, but there's people all the same. A man looks out a window at me.

There's kids in a garden throwing stones into a tree, they stop and stare as I walk past then start again. One of them skitters a rock along behind me, it hits the back of my leg and stings. I keep walking with my fists clenched. There's more of them than there is of me and I know my numbers good enough to know to stay shut-mouthed, though if they come after me I'll swing the bag of bolts, I'll crack their heads.

Round the corner, there's a mank dog. He's lying on the road, mud-streaked, wet-furred, slithery, like he's come from somewhere deep and damp. He stinks. My heart races along the road, but my feet stop, my throat closes, my breath holds. He's closed eyes. He don't see, but he knows I'm there. Black lip curls: bleeding gum, long tooth, mank breath. He snarls long and low. I step back lightly, and he's up and fierce, his eyes rolling mad. I raise the bolts, throw 'em and they scatter fly. I take off. Behind me, river dog runs, hard claws clattering, snarling throat.

I run. Dog runs faster.

The road beats upward against my feet. The world jerks. Colors I don't recognize flash past me. I can't run no more.

I stumble, arms out. I fall, and it takes an unnatural long time—too long—the falling. That's it. I'm dead. I wait for torn flesh. I lie down flat and wait to lose my neck.

There's a dull thump, and a mess of noise that is all tooth and throat and muscle and bone. I smell sour blood, I smell something's insides, but they're not mine. I risk a peek.

It's a second dog, a blur of pale yellow fur. Fighting they become one terrible snarling thing. They tumble toward me and I yelp and bury my face in the road, eyes closed, gravel pressing into my cheeks. I wait for the two of 'em to tear me apart.

And then. And then. All sound whimpers and dies. I lie there with my forehead pressed against the concrete and the only thing I can hear is my own raw breath. I dare to look. Muscle and tooth and hard nail claw—vanished. I get up warily. I look round, fists raised, ready for fighting.

The yellow dog stands to look at me from a safe distance. I can see the pale hairs of its belly, long thin scars in its short coat of matted fur. Its gut is bloated with emptiness—I know that bloat. Dog watches me. Then it turns and lopes into the yard of a broken house and disappears down the side, toward the river.

And there's just me on the long gray road. Me and the stirred-up dust and my own stuttering heart.

Market is spread out. People lay down their wares. Others pick and jumble. They come to sell and swap, they come for treasures, they come for this and that, for hum and jostle, to gather together, to tittle-tattle.

What's mine is gone, scattered on streets. I didn't have the stout to retrieve all them little pieces. My fingers aint working nohow, they're curling tight to stop 'em from shaking.

I push my way through the pickers and the crumbles, looking for Groom. But Groom aint nowhere. I ask the usuals if they seen him. They shake their heads and go back to their tattling.

"Not today, luvvy," tells Mudda Meggsy. "Buy some soap?"

"What need I got for soap?"

"You got need, girlie," Meggsy laughs. "Smells ripe you do. Look at your filth."

I sniff my forearm. "Smell like I always do."

"Listen to 'er. Dainty biscuit, you are."

People is strange—what they want, what they buy. Sometimes people what don't know better offer me paper money or silver coins in exchange for my crumbles. What good's that? I aint got no use for plinky coins. I want birds' eggs or vegetables from the ground or things for making or candles or matches. I aint got no use for much else. Paper money's for the rich, like Andrew's Doctor.

"You, girl. You. You come over here. Come and see Dolores. That's right. That's right."

At first the words is just one of market's hums, but the voice singles itself out, rising to meet me. There's a woman, older'n most, older'n Mudda Meggsy even. She wears all her clothes like some do, layers of 'em, as if they don't like to leave nothing behind. She has her wares laid out neat and nice, just a selection of things all spaced out, but not the sort of things I'd be swapping for. Dainty things, little splinters, ready to crack and brittle away, no usefulness to 'em. She aint a usual, I never seen this one afore. Sometimes ones come that just want to swap enough to keep on for a while, ones what have enough to get by otherwise, or ones what are just passing through, going somewhere else, looking for somewhere better.

I don't know her, but she looks at me. "Yes," old woman tells, all narrow and squinting. "Yes. There's waves off you all right, wobblings and tremblings. I think Dolores has something of yours."

She's scrounging round behind herself, searching through her sacks and bags. I hover and want to be gone. I think she aint quite right. Wobblings and tremblings? I meet lots that seem fine when you look at 'em but inside they're all jangled up, like their brains is full of tangles, like someone tipped out all their parts and jammed 'em back in without care.

"You aint got nothing for me, Dolores," I say. "You must be waiting on someone else. I'm looking for Groom. You know Groom?"

Dolores shakes her head and frowns, not looking round from her scrounging. "I got something for you all right. Just you wait there, girl."

Not that I'm planning on doing no waiting, but now I stopped I don't know how to walk no more. My knees is weak, like they want me to sit. My breath shakes in my body. All of a sudden I'm cold. I see in front of me, real as life, that river dog's long snarling tooth.

I crane my head looking for Groom. Where is he? How come this woman aint heard of him? Everyone round here knows Groom. I can't believe there's a person in this city that don't tattle his name. Even if there weren't no people to tell, I'd tattle it to the brown river and the low sky. Groom's older'n me, but not by much and his hands is real broad, real gentle, and his eyes is the color of the deep brown river.

"Here it is," she tells, triumphant.

"I tell you, it aint me you got for. I can't swap nothing anyway." And I spread out my empty hands.

Dolores squints. "From you, I'll take an IOU." She leans forward to offer something. It looks like a ball of glass.

"What would I be wanting this for?" I say, but I look in spite of myself and then my breath is a hook in my throat.

"Take it," she croons. "Feel the weight of it."

I hold it in my two hands and she's right, it's got weight. I feel a tight strumming in my ribs and I peer inside. There's a rough triangle of glass missing, and a sharp hole where it should be. Once the ball would have been whole and smooth, sealed up, now I can wriggle my finger inside. "It's broken," I say, and my voice creaks with disappointment, though I don't know *why* I'm disappointed. I aint buying today. I just want to find Groom. The longer the day goes the more I want to see him afore I make my long walk home.

"It's still good," she tells, persuasive. Her head bobs up and down, like she's got a loose spring. "It's still got *something*. Look, girl. Look deeper."

Inside there's a tiny girl. I seen delicate crumbles all my life, dainty little things that aint of any use, that crack away just as soon as you look and I aint never understood or desired 'em.

But the look on this girl's face carries me places. She's got her head back. I can't tell what she's doing. Her face shines, even though the world she's in is tattered and dusty. You can see that once she was with someone, there's an arm curling round her back, but the rest is gone. I wonder if they're dancing. Andrew would know. He remembers about dancing. He tried to show me once, but he said it weren't no good without music and he couldn't remember no tune to la la la.

The word *music* enters my bony skull and I turn the glass ball over. I don't know what I'm looking for, but I find it under the wooden base. It's a stiff silver key. I try to turn it, but it won't budge.

"Yes, well," Dolores tells. She's all of a sudden sharp. "Do you want it or not? I haven't got all day about it."

Neither me or Dolores has anywhere better to be. But I don't say this. Cause I want the music ball. I'm shocked with wanting it, when usually I don't want nothing but food and water and light against the dark, things what we can use. This aint of no use, there aint no call for me having it. But, yes. I want it.

"I aint got nothing," I say again. I hold on to it tightly, hold it to my chest. I think about running. She won't catch me, I know. But there's ones what marketeers pay to keep an eye for thieves—we call 'em screws—and they got fists and they got metal pipes and they can rip the hair from your scalp. And if they catch me I won't never be let to come back. Thieves aint forgotten at market, even though we're all of us making a living from taking in one way or another. *You gotta have hard lines,* Groom tells.

"I take IOUs," Dolores tells again. "But it won't be cheap."

"How do you know I'll pay?"

"Oh, you'll pay me, girl. I don't need to worry about that."

I aint dumb. I don't trust her; she's got dog's breath. Andrew would rip me if he knew I signed an IOU. But there's the girl inside the glass and I can imagine her spinning, can almost see it through a fog in my skull. I could fix that key and we could have music, Andrew and me, and maybe he could teach me real dancing. I tell myself how happy he would be if we had music, how he might wake properly, not be tired anymore. I tell myself it's for Andrew as Dolores pushes paperleaf and stub at me. I take the stub in my fist and make the letters of my name. Dolores smiles, showing her tongue, her shining teeth.

I barely finish making the last shape when suddenly there's yelling and pushing and the pointy stub snaps in my fist as the front of a man sweeps me up and propels me along in his path. Dolores snatches paper up and waves it while I'm jostled away from the table, clutching the music ball and suddenly, now that ball's mine, I feel rooked. I want my name back.

"Wait," I call. But Dolores is not in my sights no more. "Stop pushing!" I shout at the man. "I gotta get back there." But it aint no use cause it aint one man who's pushing but a jarring of bodies, all desperate to get out, clutching what's theirs.

And then, finally, through slits in the crowd of arms and bodies, I see Groom.

"Groom!" I shout, before I am lost for good in the thick of elbows.

"Clara!" He reaches out a long arm and his fingers dig into my shoulder. He yanks me though there's such a press that there aint hardly anywhere for me to go.

We push sideways against the crowd, slip through a narrow gap between old building walls and then we're running, racing down an open stretch of road, but we're going in the wrong direction from my home and eventually I stagger to a stop and turn myself round, trying to know where I am, but I don't recognize this part of the city, except to know we're somewhere near the river, I can smell the damp.

Up the road. Groom realizes I've stopped running and he stops too, leans down panting with his hands on his knees.

"Was it screws?"

He shakes his head, still out of puff. "Not screws," he gasps. "Raiders."

I hear a howl cut through the air.

"They got dogs."

I spit. Dogs. I want to kill 'em all, gristle and bone. "We gotta get back there," I say. "I gotta get home."

"Are you crazy?" Groom tells. "We aint goin back."

"I gotta get home." I stride back toward market, chin out, arms still wrapped round the damned crumble.

Groom calls after me. "Clara. They'll get you. You're just the kind of thing they like. Tasty meat."

"Aint no dog gonna eat me."

"I weren't talkin about the dogs."

I stop, but I don't turn round.

"Do you know where we are?" I say, and my voice is thin, unraveling in the empty road. The glass ball is the wrong shape for my arms. I want to put it down, that blighted box, put it on the road and walk away from it. There's something wrong about it. But I hang on to it. It's too late now. I don't know how to leave it behind.

Groom laughs. "Clara, you aint feared, are you?"

"What?"

Groom swaggers over. He looks bigger now he thinks I'm feared. "I never seen you feared."

"I been attacked by dogs and rooked by some old lady and now Raiders and more dogs and being lost." My voice quakes. I straighten my shoulders and stare fiercely at a speck of dust in the air. "I aint feared. I just want to go home."

"I'll look after you, Clara," Groom tells. He puts his arm on my shoulders. "I'll take good care."

"I don't need looking after," I tell, but I let his arm rest there a moment. My heart is pounding. Honestly I wouldn't mind being looked after by Groom. My mouth is dry as he sweeps long strands of hair out of his face so I can see his eyes. I feel the weight of the ball in my arms. "Andrew," I croak, and shrink away from Groom's embrace.

"Andrew!" Groom spits. "He keeps you. He hides you away. You need people." He touches my cheek. "You should be with me."

"We're family," I say, my cheek all a-feather where he's touched me. "Andrew'n'me."

"Aren't we family?"

I look to the depths of his brown river eyes. I shake my head regretfully.

"Well, then what? What are we?"

I can't answer. My throat is closed.

"You're cold, Clara. You're a stone-hearted girl." He grabs my shoulders, turns me round and gives me a gentle shove. I stumble forward in the direction of another street, coming off this one. "There," he tells. "Follow that. You'll find your way home, safe enough."

I stare dubiously at the street that turns into a bend afore I can see where it goes.

"This road curls back to your Andrew." Groom's voice is hard-edged. "I wouldn't steer you wrong, Clara. You know I aint lookin to harm you."

"What about you?" I say.

"What do you care?" Groom answers. Dark thoughts are scribbled all round his head.

I laugh. I can't help it.

"Don't you laugh, Clara," Groom tells. "You'll be sorry when the Raiders get me."

"No Raider's ever gonna get you," I call over my shoulder. "You're slippery as riverweed."

"Made of stone, you are," he yells. "Black-blooded."

I look back and he's still watching. I shift the weight of the glass ball and raise my hand goodbye. Soon the road bends and I know he's still there, but it don't matter if he is or not, because I'm gone.

I walk and walk and walk and I think Groom's yanked my chain once and for all because this road aint no road I never seen and I can't tell how it's gonna get me back to Andrew. But I don't know what else to do but walk it, and the road keeps crooking itself round and things seem to come together in a picture in my head and I can see like I'm a bird above—which streets are round me and where my own place is, like streets are being made while I walk, out of nothing. The road veers away from the river and I'm glad for it, but I can't stop twitching at shadows. Like I said, streets got dogs too.

I'm nearly home when one finds me. It's standing where I need to go, bigger'n life, like it's been waiting there for me. It's the yellow dog from afore, crisscrossed with belly scars. "Go on, git," I say, but dog doesn't git. I drag my voice so it's growly low, but dog just waits for me.

It steps toward me and lowers its head, its tail midheight and wagging. It means to stay. I raise my hand to strike it, swelling out my chest to make myself look bigger and fiercer. It don't flinch. It aint feared of me. When I get close I see it's got bites in its throat from that greasy river dog. Blood mats the furry ruff of its neck.

"Look," I say. "You gotta git. You know what *git* means?"

It doesn't.

"Listen. You aint mine. Andrew won't have you. Anyway, what use I got for a dog?"

The dog doesn't know that either. I sit down on the curb. It sits down beside me. I look at the glass ball in my hands. "What use I got for *this*? I must be daft-headed."

Me and the dog look at the glass ball together. The key's stuck fast. I gently coax it with my fingers, but I can't get it to turn.

"Spring must be busted," I tell the dog. I stand up, frowning at the bottom of the ball, trying to see how to open it up.

I give it one more turn and suddenly sounds come out of the box, itching the hairs inside my ears.

"Ha!" I say to dog. "I did it."

But what did I do? Each sound—ber-*ling*—is a bubble leaking from the box, shimmering and silver and oily. I don't remember Andrew telling anything like this when he telled about music and dancing; music aint nothing you're supposed to see. Maybe I even asked him when I was a little kid, and he was telling about recordings and singing and dancing, maybe I even said, openmouthed, *What does music look like?* and he would have said: *Clara, it don't look like anything, it just plink plinks, like the sound of coins or bolts rattling in your hands, only a million times better.*

But this music does look like something.

Them ber-lings come over us, me and dog. They sting my eyes and burn my skin. Dog barks and it seems like that's a bubble too, black though, not silver, oozing out of his mouth.

And then I'm somewhere new. Somewhere I aint never been afore. There's so much crowding my eyes that I can't look at nothing, cause I'm too busy looking at everything. My skin zings all over, I realize I'm cold, I'm freezing. I aint never been freezing afore. The sky is a savage color that I know is called blue, but I aint never seen blue like this. There's houses, whole and nice, and flowers, all pretty and soft and colorful growing out of rich black dirt. Everything looks polished, like Andrew's gone over the whole world with a spirit-soaked rag. The air smells sweet, and of something else, metal, manufactured. I can hear something too, a deep echoing mechanical purr, somewhere beyond the houses. The trees twitter, bursting with music of their own.

It's not till the last ber-ling's played that I remember the music and by then it's too late. Going back hurts a lot more than going there. I'm lying on the ground by the time I know where I am and the dog's licking my face. I catch a whiff of my stinking self and I think maybe at market I might do some swapping for soap after all.

I push the dog off. "You need soap too," I say, but my voice comes out dull and thudding, and bitter bile washes into my throat.

"Git," I growl. "You can't come home with me."

The dog trots off. Just like that.

"Yeah, go on," I shout. "Git. Git. I said I didn't want you nohow." My voice slaps the emptiness and rebounds.

I slither down the side of our house, through the greasy weeds. Andrew's home already, being sick on the floor.

I moon over my glass globe.

"It's called a music box, Clara." Andrew barely raises his head to look at it. He's managed to crawl to his pile and collapsed there, not getting underneath even the top layer. He don't need it, he's steaming hot.

"It aint no box," I sneer. "It's round."

Andrew stirs weakly. "That's what it's called." His voice is dry and coarse, like hands rubbing together.

"Things should only be called what they are."

Andrew drifts off again. I'm lonely. I keep fiddling with the key on the box, and then try to prise the whole thing open, but I'm feared of breaking it and that makes my fingers weak and useless. I need tools, but I need more light to use 'em by or I'd just go and lose all the tiny little screws. I'm too jittery to work nohow. But all I can care about is the fairyland. How fresh and bright it is. How alive. It's like Dolores has cursed me; like she's put a canker on my eyes and all I can see is how it is horrible here. Everything smells of vomit and piss. Andrew's being turned inside out by sickness and seeing him like that is worse than being alone. I know these aint the right feelings to have, and they aint even my feelings—not real feelings nohow. But they pluck at me, like the ber-lings, ringing in my head, and I can't think, I can't *feel,* straight.

I prowl round the rooms. I eat, Andrew doesn't. He sleeps and stirs and moans and sobs and sleeps and sicks.

I lie on my pile and burn a precious candle down to the end of its wick, watching the globe and the girl inside it. It's mine. I want to hold it so close it gets inside me. I want my skin to grow over it. I want to eat it like it's fruit. I want it to be more mine than it ever can be. It makes me feel empty, and full.

Andrew wakes. He looks like melting wax, but he's awake. "I need medicine," he rasps. He don't look at me. He makes his voice stronger in the dark. "Clara, can you hear me? I need medicine or I'll die."

"You been sick lots of times," I say, cruel-hearted with fear. "You been sick and you aint dead. You just got bugs in your stomach is all."

"I've been sick for days now, Clara. I'm not getting better. This isn't a usual bug or you'd be sick too. It's an infection. My kidney or my stomach . . . I need antibiotics. Doctor . . ."

"Doctor won't give 'em to *me*."

"He might. He might if it's for me. I'll write it down. I'll work for it. He knows I'm a good worker."

"You're gonna write an IOU?" My voice is shrill as a cockroach's in the dark.

"Please, Clara." Andrew collapses back on his pile. "Just get paper."

"What paper?"

"The book. The one you brought home the other day. That'll do."

"You're gonna rip it?" Andrew don't rip books nor use 'em to make fire.

"Clara, do you hear me? I'm going to *die* if I don't get medicine."

I get the book, stomping through the house, making as

much noise as possible. I rip out a page myself, choosing so carefully that Andrew snaps me again for being so bloody-headed. He writes it with a stub from his pocket. "Can you read that?"

On one side is his IOU. On the other he's written a long word, so long the letters jumble together and I can't separate them out. He sounds it out for me. *"An-ti-bi-o-tics."*

"You aint gonna die," I say, folding the piece of paper carefully and stashing it. "This is stupid cause you aint gonna die. But I'll go get your antibiotics for you. And you'll be sorry slaving for Doctor for nothing."

"Fine," Andrew tells. "I'll be sorry. Thank you, Clara."

"It's dark outside," I say, in a different voice. And then, "Don't die. Don't."

Andrew's gone again. The sickness has taken him back.

There's a moon out, its face as pale and sickly in the gray night as Andrew's. These streets I know well, but it's slow going in the pitch of the night and my heart thrums in my chest. As I approach Doctor's house I hear voices and tinkling and I see glows of light coming from the windows. Doctor's entertaining.

I crouch and peep in. The smell of their drinks is as stomach-churning as the Raiders, though they hold their glasses dainty as though they contain something fine. I see Doctor, red-faced and plump. He is the only one of them who is plump. But they need him, Andrew tells, so he fills his belly first and gets the best pickings. Most of 'em look blurry, like what they're drinking is making 'em soft and pulpy. Those closest to him look a little feared.

I stand. What am I hiding for? I need to be seen, need to talk to Doctor. And I aint feared. I aint never been feared.

Someone grabs my arm. "C'mon, you," he tells. "This aint no fancy do for the likes of you."

I twist my arm, but he holds tight, his fingers digging through muscle into bone. "I gotta see Doctor."

Man laughs. "Doctor don't wanna see you, boy. Then again"—he wheezes sulfur breath in my face—"he might. He likes 'em small."

"I'm no boy!"

"A girl, are ya?" He grabs my chin and pushes my face toward the light. "For sure he don't wanna see you. An' who would? You is skankier than a bag of rats' balls. He likes 'em clean."

"I aint come to be looked at. It's this he wants to see," I say, waving the piece of paper.

"What's that then?"

I snatch it away. "It aint for the likes of *you*. It's business."

"Oh ho. Business, izzit? What business does a squeak like you got for a Boss like him?"

"It aint me got business. 'Nother Boss sent me."

"Sent a little girl in the middle of the night? With the Raiders out?" His lip curls like river dog's, but he got less teeth.

I sigh and shake my head. "He don't care about no Raiders. He's cruel, my Boss."

"Must be." Man flicks me away. "All right. You go see

Doctor or don't, it's same same to me. But don't tell him I saw you or nothin'. I could break you into bits if I want."

I slink inside, keeping close to the walls. Doctor is talking large. I aint feared of nothing, but if I were, I'd be feared of Doctor. Andrew don't tell much about him, but I know Doctor knows how to hurt as well as to heal, how to make pain last. As much as I want to I can't disappear—I can't. I step out into the room. Hardly no one notices me at first. Then three of 'em, two men, one lady, peer down at me.

"Look at this," one man tells. He is exceptional tall. "Isn't it a tiny, dirty thing?"

"It came from the shadows." The other man leans toward me.

"Is it made of shadows?" asks the first.

"Is it real?" asks the second, his eyes bright but empty. "Is it pretend?"

"Hush, Duguld, Brown. It's a little stray child. It's scared. Come here. Are you a boy or a girl? Oh, a little girl!" She is wearing something red and furry and rumpled, soft-lookin', and so clean it could be from the fairyland. I want to touch it. I clutch my fingers behind me. "Do you like it?" The lady strokes her coat. "It's called velvet. You can touch it if you want." The Velvet Lady draws me closer. With one finger I touch her coat. One way smooth, the other way rough.

"I aint stray," I say. "And I aint feared."

"Now, now." The Velvet Lady laughs, as though I please her in some way. "Manners. Even in times like these there is always cause for manners."

"I need to see Doctor."

"Come now," the lady insists, amused. "Let me walk you out. One of these gentlemen—this is Brown, and this is Duguld—will escort us. They are more effective than they appear."

"I need to see Doctor," I say, sulky, and cause I know what *manners* means, I add, *"Please."*

"You need not to see the Doctor," the man Duguld tells, "is what you need."

"Andrew's sick. He needs medicine."

"Doctor's boy?" Brown asks. His face goes sharp.

I nod, though it sicks my insides to call Andrew "Doctor's." Andrew's mine. Not anyone else's.

The lady and the men look at each other. "I'll take her." The lady isn't teasing no more. "Come on. What's your name?"

"Clara."

"I'll introduce you, Clara. I warn you, he won't like you being here tonight. And do remember your manners. He likes a clean tongue. Pity there's nothing we can do about your face. But he's fond of Andrew. In his way." She's holding my elbow, guiding me through the party. People step away from us and mutter. "Horace, this is Clara," Velvet Lady tells, softly. "She's here to see you about—"

Doctor don't even look. "Put it away. It's not wanted here."

"It's about your boy, Andrew." The Velvet Lady's voice is almost a whisper.

"Please," I tell. "He wanted me to give you this." I hold up the piece of paper.

"Andrew?" He gazes round the room. He's putting on a show. "Tell him he's fired. I can't have my workers taking days off whenever it suits them."

"He's sick. He's real sick. He needs medicine. Anti . . . antibiotics. Else he'll die."

I see something in Doctor's face. Lady's right. He is fond of Andrew. In his way.

"I got an IOU," I push. "He'll work for nothing, as long as you want him to."

Everyone's stopped their muttering and is watching instead. His face hardens to bone. "And if I give him medicine and he dies anyway? What good is this contract to me if he's dead?"

He won't take the paper from my hand. And I realize what a mistake I've made. If he'd been alone, maybe he would've done it. Maybe. But not with an audience he won't. Not when he's entertaining.

"You can have me," I say.

He laughs. "And what use would you be?"

"And Groom." I apologize to Groom in my head. "I can get Groom. He'll help. If I ask him, he'll work for you too." I am sure this weren't true, but I have nothing else to offer.

"Who or *what* is Groom?" Doctor's playing with me, like river dog plays with river rat, tossing it into the air, rattling its bones to break its neck.

"He's Boss. He's Boss like you." The lie slithers off my tongue. "Boss of market. Boss of the Zone."

"A dead man, a soiled girl-infant and market scum? This is all you have to offer?"

Laughter ripples round the room.

"Do you know what some of these people have paid me? Do you know what the going rate is for a simple cough elixir, let alone antibiotics? Do you know nothing about the nature of the world in which you reside?"

"Please. Please. It's Andrew I'm asking for." I nearly choke. "Your boy."

Doctor looks at me again, as if I'm a rat on a plate. "So you're the little thing he goes home to every night. Can't say I see the appeal myself." He holds out his empty glass and a man quickly fills it with firewater. "He ever tell you that I asked him to live here, with me?"

I nod.

"Think about that then. If he were here, he'd have a doctor on call twenty-four hours a day. Fresh fruit and vegetables. Clean water. He'd never get sick." He sips his nasty drink. "Seems to me the one who has signed his death certificate, child, is you."

The Velvet Lady is quick to grab at my arms, but I'm quicker. I use her to hold my weight as I kick as high as I can with both legs, propelling him backward. My foot connects with his nose and there's a satisfying crack. Blood spurts. His face twists with rage. I spit at him and scream and fight, trying to get at him, but he's got protection—two men descend and I'm dragged out of the Lady's arms, toward the door.

"He aint your boy!" I shout, and I know Doctor's listening. So's everyone at the party. "He aint your boy. He's mine and you know it. You want him, but I got him. I'm family. You're nothing to him! You want to think you're something, but you're *nothing*. That's why he aint here."

They throw me down and kick me with boots and leave me broken in the road, but not dead. I hold my head, even after they've gone. I don't feel nothing in my bones or skin, but inside I'm howling at that watery moon like the fiercest river dog. When I open my eyes, Brown, Duguld and the Velvet Lady are standing over me. The Velvet Lady bends over and plucks the IOU from my hand.

"Pretty words," she tells, reading it. "What a shame. I do like Andrew."

"Do you still want to keep it?" Brown asks, bored, touching me with his foot.

"It's broken." Duguld's face is sour.

"She's dangerous," the Velvet Lady tells. She sighs, as though she really was planning to keep me. "She'd get me into trouble."

"What's it going to do?" asks Brown.

"Horace won't help her now, that's for certain. She'll have to look somewhere else."

"*Is* there anywhere else?" asks Duguld.

"Where do you think Horace gets his medicine from? Marketeers and Raiders and traffickers and traders."

"Us?"

"We can't help her. Not now. It would mean strife."

"War," tells Brown, glum.

"She'll have to find another way. It will cost her though. She'll need to be cannier than she was with Horace. Not just sharp-tongued. She'll need to be sharp all over."

"That little dusty thing? It's got no hope."

The Velvet Lady stares down at me and I can't tell by her face what she's thinking. She tells Brown and Duguld, "Come on, then. I think it's time you took me home."

"Is the party over?" asks Duguld.

"I've had enough of Horace for one night." The Velvet Lady leans down. "Good night, Clara girl," she tells, tucking the IOU into my hand. "Here. Take these pretty, careless words. Someone needs to teach you two the art of drawing up a contract. The trick is, be specific."

I stir. "Thank you," I murmur.

"Good girl. That's what you need. Manners. You'll go a long way with manners." She looks at me and pulls something out from inside her velvet. It's a little gold stick. She uncaps it and twists the end. It's for painting lips, there's ones what sell 'em at market. She leans down and swirls it on my forehead. I reach up to touch. "Leave it," she tells. "I can't help you with what you're looking for, but this will show you have my protection. You'll be left alone tonight."

I pull myself upright. My bones are sore and my skin is torn. I ache all over, but I've had worse. I'm ready to keep moving. I'm closer to market than home and, after Doctor, aint nothing afears me, 'cept going home without medicine, to watch Andrew die. And someone at market might have what I need. If anyone knows, Groom does. So I'm gonna go to market. I'm gonna find Groom.

Groom's right. Night markets is different. There's an oily stench to it. I can feel it seeping into my skin. There's little lights all over, in between great spreading patches of dark. Night markets has a noise too, drumming. It's hard and fast and it makes my heart beat faster to match, makes me edgier, makes the darkness jump out at me.

There's knots of people making their swaps, though what's selling and what's buying aint clear, nothing's laid out, as far as I can see. There's not the twitter of daytime tattling, there's not the thrum and the jostle. It's serious. It's business.

Not everyone's making sales though. There's little circles of people all over with metal pipes, sticking 'em into little pots of fires and breathing up the smoke. Some of 'em slump over straightaway, some stare into the flames. They twitch and giggle, or cry, or grind their jaws, their eyes dancing flames. I can see they aint gonna be no use to me.

I go up to a woman. She's sitting at a table with a lamp on it, that's all. She's gazing into the darkness, and she don't seem to have nothing to sell. "Where's Groom?" I ask her.

"Who is this Groom when he's at home? You aint the first what's asked me today. Oh, it's you again."

It's Dolores, the one what swapped me the globe. The one what's got my name in her creeping claw.

"Come to pay up already? No, no. Not yet. Soon. But here, girl, how's about a fortune. Cross my palm with silver."

"I aint got no silver," I snap. I don't want no hocus fortune.

"Don't want to know what the future's gonna bring? My old mother back there, in the tent, she knows everything. Don't you, Mum? She told me all about you."

I hear an ancient voice creaking in the darkness, even older than Dolores, almost all used up. "Hard to enthuse on recent efforts. Mixing form and proving hard to follow. Bled during race. Look to others. Wait until she shows more."

"Come on now, a fortune. On the house for a loyal customer."

"No." I force myself to add, "Thank you," remembering my manners like the Velvet Lady told me.

"Oh very nice, milktongue." She squints at me. "I see you got *'er* mark. We aint friends, 'er and me. But you'll be needing it tonight."

"Look to others," the tent-voice creaks.

"Yes, Mum, you said that one already. I'll see you, Clara girl. See you again before mornin', no doubt."

I follow the sound of the drums. It's getting louder and faster and people are shouting. When I get closer there's a shape looming in the darkness, a huge makeshift structure made of wood and cloth, and there's men at the gaping door—screws—taking tickets and roughing up those that try and sneak through without one.

I stand back, trying to see what's what, scoping another way in.

Someone grabs my hair before I can reach the door. "'Allo, girlie."

I can't pull free. I twist. It aint no screw. I just manage to gander a boy—no, a man, all scrawn, and no hair, only skin on his tight head.

"Whatchoo lookin' for?"

"Groom," I snap. "He's a friend of mine."

"Groom, eh?" His grip loosens, but he don't let go. "Well now, I wouldn't want to bruise no fruit of Groom's."

"I aint no fruit."

"Is that right, girlie? Well, Groom, see . . . I happen to know he's busy. He's real busy. Best you let old Pip here look after ya, until Groom gets back. I'll treat ya real nice, see?

Not a mark. Though maybe"—he reaches out and plucks out a hair—"maybe I'll take a hair or two. Just a little memento, see?"

"Let me go."

He plucks another and sniffs it. "You need washin'. I got soap. Let Pip do for ya."

I twist, searching out Groom. "Why's everyone got themselves lathered about soap all of a sudden?"

"Who else wants to wash ya?" Pip groans, pressing his cheek against mine, his fingers tangling tighter in my hair. "We's could wash you together. I'm a sharin' man, Pip."

My stomach rises. He's foul. "Oh, you wouldn't know him. He aint so into sharing. His name's Doctor. Only I call him Horace. It's him what sent me here to find Groom. Business."

Pip drops my hair like it's snakes. "Doctor? I thought . . . You gotta forget the name Pip. Or on second thoughts, maybe I should forget for ya. Little snip on ya head should do it." I hear the flick of a knife. "Carve it right out." I spin round, fists raised, ready to fight.

There's a low growl. I look down and it's the dog.

"You got a dog?" Pip tells. "What are ya, a Raider?" That's when he sees the mark on my forehead and staggers back, looking round over his shoulders. He looks feared now. "You are! You aint gonna get *her* onto me?" he whines. "I was nice, right? I only took a hair."

"You took two," I spit, rubbing my scalp. Dog advances.

"But I didn't hurt ya none." He backs away. "I didn't hurt ya."

"Where's Groom?" I say.

Pip gestures toward the drumming. "In there." He leers again, and his face makes me sick in my guts.

Dog barks and Pip turns and runs into the black, tripping over a group of pipe-blowers and almost falling into their fire.

"Hello, dog. Where you come from? Didn't I tell you to git?" Dog presses its body against my legs. It's warm. Its wagging tail beats against me. I smooth down the fur on its head. "Let's find Groom."

At the tent door I'm stopped. "Can't go in without a ticket," screw tells. "Anyway, it aint fer you. I got daughters and I wouldn't let them in there neither. You wanna keep safe elsewhere, my love. You trust Ole John."

"I need to see Groom."

"You don't wanna see him now, girlie," tells another screw, with a nasty grin. "He's busy."

The drumming climaxes again and a roar rises out of the tent.

"Burstin time," Ole John tells to the screw with the nasty grin. "Go in and get young Groom, Juzzy."

"What for?" Juzzy spits. "We do for what kiddies tell us now? We aint got enough Bosses?"

"She got a Boss's mark. Look at her forehead."

Still grumbling, Juzzy goes inside.

Takes him a long time. Afore he comes back there's a wooden cage carried inside. I crane my neck, but Ole John pulls me away. Dog growls faint and low. "This aint no kiddie circus," Ole John warns. "It aint nice." He nods at the dog. "Good chap you got there. Reminds me of a shep I had when I was a boy, used to come from miles away when I whistled. But that was before. You wouldn't remember that, would you? Too young. Even Juzzy in there were jus' a spring lamb. This aint no world to be bringing up kiddies, that's fer blinking sure."

Juzzy leads Groom out. When Groom sees me he looks down, small and shamed. His cheeks are colored and his eyes dart away like black mice in a room, sliding from one shadow to another, not fixing on me. A tall thin silver girl's arm is wrapped round his neck, she's whispering in his ear, her hand creeping down to his privates. My stomach twists. Groom shrugs her away. She don't seem to care much. She pouts and moves on to Ole John, trying to wind her arms round him, but he pats her kindly on the back and pushes her toward the opening. I notice Ole John don't check *her* ticket, maybe she's part of the show.

"Clara! What are you doin here? What happened to you?" Groom grabs my arm and drags me away. I glance back at the tent to remember my manners, but Ole John and Juzzy is busy taking tickets and seeing others out. It seems one show's ended and another's about to begin.

"What's in there?" I ask. "What's bursting time?"

"Why you here, Clara? If I'd known you were comin, I'd a looked after you. Did you get beat up? Night markets isn't for wanderin alone."

"I don't need looking after," I snap. He looks wounded. "I need medicine."

"You sick?" He looks at dog in disgust. "What's that? You keepin dogs now, Clara?"

"I didn't feed it or nothing. Just keeps showing up when it's needed. Unlike some."

"That aint fair."

"Sorry." I wobble on my feet.

"Clara? You are sick!" Groom pulls me down to sit on the hard ground under a lantern hanging in a tree. He wraps an arm round me and squeezes me. It's nice. I like it. I want to stay like this, to rest against his chest. But I think of the silver girl wrapped round his neck and I pull away.

"No, I aint sick. Just tired."

"Come with me. I'll take you to the Zone and you can sleep awhile. I'll make up a bed for you, warm as a nest, and bring you honey on a spoon."

"Can't sleep. Need medicine. Andrew's sick."

"Andrew! *He* sent you out in the dark?"

"He didn't even know it were dark. He's dying, aint he? He sent me to Doctor."

"You went to Doctor's house? Clara, are you cracked?"

"He wouldn't give it to me."

"I coulda told you he wouldn't and saved you a trip!"

"He would have. Andrew's his favorite. But he was entertaining."

"You cut his party? You are cracked. Did he kill you?"

"I kicked his nose. And spit in his eye."

Groom leaps up and paces. The dog watches him, back and forth, back and forth. "Clara, Clara," he groans. "What are you doin to me?"

"I aint doing nothing to you. This is about Andrew. I gotta get him well."

"What's he need? What sort of medicine?"

"Antibiotics."

Groom shakes his head. "You won't get 'em here. I'm sorry, Clara."

"What? You can't know that! You gotta check first. Ask round. *Someone's* got 'em."

"This is my market. Trust me, I know. There's no line for that sort of medicine here. It don't have the effect the punters want, know what I'm sayin? You saw 'em. The sniffers and the blowers. They aint lookin to get well. They're lookin to get high."

"What about people in the Zone?"

"People in the Zone get sick they stay sick. Unless they got an in with Doctor."

"But the lady said—"

"What lady?"

"The Velvet Lady. She said—"

"Velvet?"

"She wore a . . ." I brush my shoulders.

"Cloak?"

I nod. "She painted this on my forehead."

Groom kneels down beside me, his eyes blazing as he tilts my head into the light. "You met Boedica?"

"She didn't tell her name."

"The Velvet Lady!" Groom shakes his head. "Clara, you know who she is?"

I close my eyes. Darkness swims. I need sleep. The dog presses itself against me again and I put a hand on its back to steady myself. I shake my head no.

"She's a Raider!"

"She weren't no Raider. She were nice, I think. She talked posh, like Andrew."

"She's a Raider. She's *the* Raider. She's Boss. She's bigger Boss than Doctor even, some would say. That's probably why you weren't killed for breakin Doctor's nose."

"She told me to mind my manners."

Groom laughs. "Trust you to get Boedica's mark. But listen, Clara. She aint nice. Don't let her fool you into thinkin that. She's given you somethin, she's gonna want somethin in return."

"She said marketeers. This is where Doctor gets his medicine."

"I know where Doctor gets his medicine," Groom tells. "Or some of it anyways. Clara, they aint gonna be found unless they wanna be found. And they don't wanna be found. Besides, they deal in money. Where you gonna get money?"

"You telling me it's impossible?"

"Well, with my contacts"—Groom puffs himself up—"maybe in a week or two . . ."

"A week or two! He'll be dead by then." I stare at Groom. "You just don't want to help cause it's Andrew. You want him to die."

"You know that aint right."

"You just want to *keep* me. You're as bad as Pip."

"Pip?"

"He said I was your fruit."

"Fruit? What are you gabblin, Clara? You're all tangled."

I stand. I aint wasting no more time. "I gotta go."

"Stay until mornin. It aint safe."

"I got dog. It looks after me. And I got this mark."

"You got Andrew. You got the dog." Groom's voice strains against the dark. "You got Boedica's mark. You don't need me."

"I did need you. Didn't I? I asked. But you won't help."

"Not won't. Can't."

"I gotta go. If I can't . . . if I can't get medicine, then I gotta at least . . . go home."

Groom grabs my hand. "If it were me who were sick, would you look after me? Would you get medicine?"

"You got the silver girl for that," I say, black-hearted. "I'm for Andrew and he's for me. He never asked nothing from me afore, he's only ever always looked after me, like he were a brother or a father. Andrew's what's mine."

"I'm yours too, you just gotta say. I'm more yours than any brother. Will you have me, Clara?"

"I won't."

"Clara! Please. You know I'd get antibiotics if I could. But I aint the all-powerful you think I am. If that Velvet Lady can't get 'em to you, aint no one who can."

I feel dog's breath on my ankles, as I stride away from Groom's light, into the dark. And I feel, pressing against my eyes, the burning salt of tears. Aint no mark to protect me from what I feel, but I wish there were all the same.

"She's lookin' in all the wrong places. Isn't that right, Mum?" Dolores's voice floats out of the darkness. I've passed her table, but I stop. Dog's fur bristles. "You're not gonna get them pills you want from here. You gotta go back *there*."

"Back to Doctor? He won't never give 'em to me. Not after I kicked him."

"You kicked Horace?" She rasps a laugh. "Hear that, Mum?"

"Expect bold showing," the tent-voice behind her creaks.

"So you said, Mum, so you said. In the money, you reckon?"

"Shows strong stable."

"You heard her. Straight from the horse's mouth, so to speak." Dolores chuckles wheezily. "No, no. Not Doctor's. Take it from me," she lulls, "you want to go back *there*. Didn't old Dolores give you the key, just this morning?"

"To fairyland?"

"Fairyland?" Dolores wheezes again. "That's right, that's right. You turned the key, didn't you? You opened the door?"

"There was no door," I mutter. "There was bubbles. Leaky bubbles."

"You didn't do it right, did you? She didn't do it right, hey Mum?"

"Chance with suitable conditions. Needs more ground."

"There you go. Can't get clearer than that."

I can barely see Dolores. Her lantern is out, there's only the light from the tent and her mother's dark shape. The night presses in, there aint no moon no more. I peer into the darkness. Is she unsprung?

"But how am I s'posed to get back there? How am I s'posed to stay long enough to find medicine? I was in and out, soon as the music stopped."

"You gotta walk through the door. But you need the key.

You always need the key." She strikes a fizzing match and lights her lantern again. "You go along now, girl. I'll get Mum hunkered down, then I'll follow along behind. You'll be gone and back in a blink of an eye and then we can settle up. Now, mind me. You know what happens to little girls who don't pay what they owe, don't you?"

I don't know. But the voice in the tent creaks like an old bird, "Scratched. Scratched. Scratched."

"That mark on your forehead won't protect you from everything. Boedica don't frighten me none. I got powers of my own. Now, off you go, quicksmart." She leans down to dog, holding up her lantern. "Dog'll snuffle them out for you, all right, won't you, Devil? You've got the scent, don't you? 'Andsome fellow, that you are." Dog raises a lip and growls at her. Dolores raises a lip and growls back. "Now listen, girlie. You get this one little thing and that's all. You can't go snatching willy-nilly this and that or everything will be turvy-topsy, all fall down. Just take a little at a time, just the skim of a skerrick, a bit o' nothing out of all that plenty and no one will be noticing, but go hauling and carting . . . well. There are rules for thieving. This aint no lawful quarry, in empty hearths. You is taking something, just a little something and no harm done, but taking all the same."

I nod. I aint altogether comfortable with thieving, cause Andrew always insisted not if we can live at being honest, but what use is goodliness in this case? No harm done, like Dolores tells. Just a little something from plenty, what won't be missed, and I will have Andrew back, to tell me how it's wrong.

Dog and I leave the territories of market. We walk back through the dark and we're left untroubled. Raiders is quiet tonight, and I got the mark. The night is long. Morning aint nowhere near even though I feel like I've lived two long nights already. Night of Doctor and the Velvet Lady, one. Night of Pip and the Screws, Dolores and Market and Groom, two. And now another's starting.

I'm puzzling over what Dolores tells. The key and the door. I guess the key is the wind-up on the music box. I aint worried about the key, 'cept I'll have to budge it again. But where's the door? And how much more will I owe? If I use the music box to save Andrew's life, will Dolores's price go up? I don't even know what she wants in return, but I reckon I'm getting pulled further and further into her darkness.

When I get home I tell dog to wait while I get the key. I lean down and ruffle its fur, one way smooth, one way rough, like the Lady Boedica's cloak.

Andrew's yellow and breathing. He wakes when I come in, leastways his eyes open, but he don't see nothing, or maybe it aint Andrew looking out no more. I step over him to get the music box, but he grabs my ankle.

"There's someone upstairs," he tells. "I can hear them walking around."

I shake him off. "There aint no one there, it's just being sick makes you hear things. Go back to sleep."

"Shuffle shuffle. Sad steps. Like she's wearing slippers. Remember slippers? And a warm dressing gown that's been hanging near the heater while you have your bath? Milk and raisins and stories before bed?"

"No."

He listens. "She's looking for you, but she can never find you."

"She aint looking for me. Aint no one looking for me." I grab the music box. "Listen. I gotta go out. Your Doctor didn't want to help you none, and the Raiders and Groom weren't no help neither. So I gotta try somethin' else."

Andrew tries to sit up. "I can hear music. Can you hear it, Clara? It's sweet. It hurts."

"No. I can't. Did you hear me? I gotta go."

"It's coming from upstairs." He makes a humming sound and I recognize the tune. I look up at the ceiling. Music? A key and a door. The locked room upstairs—is that what Dolores was telling?

The music makes Andrew whimper. Then he falls quiet.

I kneel down and wipe the slick from his forehead. He blinks. "Clara?" he asks foggily. "Is that you? Are you home?"

"Not yet," I tell. "Soon."

Andrew closes his eyes and goes back to proper sleep. I take the music box, some candles and my little box of tools and parts I use for the crumbles. I shut the door behind me.

"Well, dog. We gotta go up. You know what up is?"

If dog does, then it don't know any better'n me how to get to that room. Dolores's old mother was right about something, anyways. I need more ground.

I find a sheltered part in the front of the house and light a candle.

"First things first. Door aint no use if I aint got no key," I say.

I unscrew the wooden base of the box and find the mechanism inside, cogs and a little metal pipe with pins sticking out and a little sliver of metal that spins to turn the cogs. There's a metal casing and this unscrews too. It's tricky work by candlelight and I gotta be real careful about where I put the little tiny screws, tipping 'em into the scooped bowl of the wooden base. I see the problem, there's a piece of ribbon, metal and fine, flapping, when it should be coiled like a spring. I carefully loop it back. The last trick is to catch the little eye on the end through the hook in the casing to hold the spring in place. Then I screw it all back together.

"Let's see if it works," I tell dog. Dog is too busy running all over, sniffing every little thing, to answer. I give the music box one small wind. The key turns real easy, real nice in my finger and thumb. Dog barks as visible blobs of music squeeze out of the box and float up. Fat leaky bubbles, dripping silver oil. One brushes my skin. "Ouch!" I say, and shake my hand, but the stinging doesn't stop.

When I look straight through the bubbles, I can see fairyland, though this time me and dog stay in this world. All the bubbles are drawn up to the second floor and in their wake a way up ripples into being, flickering against the air. "That's called a staircase, that is," I tell dog. "You coming up? We better be quick. It don't look too solid."

I run up the stairs that the music bubbles have left glimmering in their trail. The bubbles pop against the internal wall, the music is fading and the magic with it. Dog stands at the bottom of the staircase and whines. "Come on, dog, you heard Dolores. She said we had to stay together." Dog steps onto the staircase, but the staircase is already wavering as the bubbles drift away. "Come on, quick," I call. I remember Ole John and his shep. I whistle, long and loud. Dog runs up toward me. Stair by stair, the staircase vanishes behind dog as it runs up. But the staircase is vanishing from the top too, at my feet. "Jump!" I shout when it's near the top. Only three steps remain, hanging in the middle of space. Dog leaps over darkness and lands on its front legs, nearly slipping. It scrabbles up and I heave it, just as the music stops.

We peer at the candle we've left flickering downstairs. "Well, hopefully that trick'll work again," I say. "It's a long way down." I rub my arm. It's raw and stinging from where the bubble grazed me.

The floorboards at my feet is spongy, so I feel across with my feet and make sure to walk only where supporting beams are. "You follow right along behind me, dog," I say. "I aint nursing two patients." Dog's good company. Even if it don't talk back, the sound of my own voice makes me brave.

We make our way like this, edging along in the almost dark (morning's closer, darkness is speckling, like it's separating into dust) to the door of a locked upstairs room. I jiggle the handle and it won't budge. I look round for something to bash against it, but I don't know how I'm gonna do that when I have to balance where the stupid beams are.

"Well, I got the key. And I got a door. Now what?" Dog looks at me as if my head's stuffed with feathers. "I use the key to open the door? Now, why didn't I think of that?" I turn the key in the music box, winding it round and round. There's bubbles and bubbles this time, the music glides out of the box and sticks to the door, and the door shimmers toxic silver. Behind me is still rubble and dust. I try the handle again, and it burns at my skin. I pull my hand away. I breathe and try a third time. It feels like my skin is blistering with that poisonous music, but I clench my teeth. The handle slips round easy enough.

"Come on, dog, you're with me, right?" I reach down and gently squeeze its neck scruff. "Well, yeah, it's gonna hurt. Course it is. Gonna hurt worse than any of them greasy bubbles. But we gotta do this. We aint got no choices now."

And I push open that silver door, my eyes squeezed tight, and step inside.

Claire feels the breach like the opening of a wound: flesh separating to let the air in (and with it the poisons and scents of the world) and to let the insides leak out (bad blood and good, mingled, indivisible).

Clara enters and the dream enters. Claire's dream expands so she is also dreaming herself. She is dreaming a shadow of herself, who is dreaming.

The music that Clara carries, that stepped her from one world into another, threatens the borders of Claire, oozing both in and out of the dream—two musics, rising with violence to meet each other. Clara steps toward Claire and almost touches her hair. And Claire could wake now, could rise with violence or hope or love, to meet herself, her other. Could wake, couldn't she? And meet Clara in the eye. If she chose.

The dog is also there. The dog is the realest thing in the

room. It is the dog that stops Claire leaking into Clara, or Clara drifting into Claire.

Clara has breached the divide, the borders of dreaming, and deep inside her dream Claire hopes that whatever happens in the dream happens here too. If Clara saves Andrew, then Charlie might also be saved. So Claire plays her small part, and stays steadfastly asleep, however tempting it is to wake herself, to step out of the dream and into one world or another or both, straddling the gap, like Clara.

It's unnatural how deeply she sleeps. I aint never seen anyone sleep like that, so still and wax, like a crumble with glass eyes—only I can't see her eyes, can I, cause she's sleeping. Is this how they sleep in fairyland? Up high off the floor, atop a soft thing only made for sleeping in. All rumpled in pillows and blankets, all buried, except for her nose to breathe through, except for her streaming hair. I want to touch her hair, but when I reach toward her the dog wuffles. She don't wake or nothing, but I pull away all the same.

I press my finger to my lips.

"Shut-mouthed," I whisper.

I look round the room. What a lot of surfaces she's got, what a lot of things. Everything laid out as if it were precious, as if it were treasure. My eyes can't stick to any of it, it's like market when it's all laid out, but there aint nothing you want. None of it aint worth looking at, not properly. Everything is treasure and nothing is, that's what Andrew tells times he's joined me at market.

There aint medicine here. She's sleeping, but look at her, she's pink-mouthed and damp-lashed, soft-cheeked and gentle-breathed. She aint sick. In fact, she's so healthy it seems she's got her own light hazing off her, and I marvel at this till I see it's from the window behind her that the light enters the room.

I push back the window hangings. There's baubles of light threaded all up and down the world, like giant twinkly candles, warm and yellow. I could stand here forever, glassed in, watching the bluish night spreading out. My bones are turning to liquid. But I can't stop.

"I can't stop," I say to dog. It's glad about that. It wants to go out. It's an outside dog, it is. It don't belong in no queenly room, with all this crowding of things. It whines and pads back to the doorway, now just a dark hole, the silver music all dried up.

"That way?" I ask it. "How do we know it won't just take us back?" Dog walks through the hole and stands on the other side. I clear a space on one of them surfaces and put the music crumble onto it. "It's safer here," I tell dog. My arms float free without it, I been hugging that thing so tight.

Dog leads me down a hallway made of long lines. Rooms—whole rooms, nothing broken—come off one side and the other. I stop at one of them. The door is half open so one space tiptoes into another. I tremble. There is someone deep and musky breathing sleep in there. Someone powerful and gentle just the same.

Dog barks again.

"Shut it," I hiss, but I follow. Oh the stairs, how substantial they feel beneath our feet, how whole and good. Each one is its own territory stepping down to become another and then another. How neatly they lock together, like mechanical insides, as though they are the workings for the house.

Dog seems to know where it's going. It'll sniff 'em out, Dolores said. So I follow it, and when it scratches at the front door I open it wide.

Out. The night is airy blue and there's those yellow globes of light and high high high in the stretched-out sky there's pricks of white. The air is wet with chill. Dog is running round sniffing and weeing and having itself a fine time.

"Where do we go now, dog?" I hiss.

Dog takes one last sniff, then trots off. I jump over a groomed strip of vegetable, from one place to the next, and follow him. It's snuffling its nose deep into some pot of something, it scrapes with its paw, until I take over and I uncover it. A key glints in the black soil. I scrape the dirt from its ridges and ease it into the silver lock and turn it.

Dog sits on the threshold. I grab its scruff. "Come on." But it won't budge. I step in alone. I'll have to sniff 'em out myself. I follow my nose, past one open door, to another.

Wafting out of this room is two smells at once, one on top of the other. One is high and sharp, a clean smell what Andrew brings back with him from Doctor's. The other is flat and soiled and I can taste it in my throat. It's the smell of a body gone bad. It's the smell of Andrew as he is now, the smell of sickness and oozings and death.

I creep in.

Under the heavy pile of blankets is a human lump, living and dying at the same time.

I edge along the bed. This aint a room of things. There's one table with a smattering of what's needed by someone too gone to *want,* a glass of water for sipping and . . . My hand reaches forward and grabs a squatting white bottle. Medicine. I knock the glass of water to the floor.

The human thing sits up. She grips my wrist in a bony claw. She looks right at me, but she doesn't see me. She aint awake, or sleeping. She's dreaming, but I'm her dream. She's reached out to take dreaming by the wrist, to rattle a dream's bones.

"Scratched!" she shrieks. "Scratched! Scratched! Scratched!"

I pull my wrist free and run. The medicine rattles in its bottle. I run like there's Raiders chasing me, and Doctor's gang and screws and all, like they're all on my tail.

"Dog!" I hiss into the garden air as loud as I can let, but dog's gone. "Dog! Dog!"

I whirl round. I grieve after it, cold air howls in the hollowness of me, but dog's gone. A sudden yellow light opens out into the night. I aint got time. I say it. "I aint got time for this, dog." But it don't come bounding out of the shadows. Dog's gone.

I run up them stairs: I don't care how neatly put together they are, how they is made of straight lines like the insides of the music box. I got what I wanted, didn't I? Dog's better off here than scrounging after me, and I shut my heart to the grief of losing it. There is noises downstairs, a flurry of rush in the night, a voice like Dolores, but soft and frightened, questioning the darkness.

"Hello? Are you there? Who's there? Who's there?" Who who, like a nightwing hunting in the river's overgrowth.

As I pause outside the half-open door, I hear something stir. Whatever breathed deep in there is awake now, and about to rise and discover me. I want to be discovered—half—I want my knees to give in and collapse beneath me. I want whatever gentle, powerful thing dwells in that darkness to carry me down. But Andrew. Andrew.

I scuttle back to the girl's room, and gently click the latch into place, and lean against her door, air scraping my lungs.

I pick up the music box. It's heavier'n afore. I take it over to the windowlight and look deep into the box and, by some hexery, it's fixed. The girl in there, in that world of glass, she aint alone no more. She's still dancing, but she's got a partner—a gentleman mouse, if you please! I seen such things in the treasures: stories Andrew makes for me. He is dressed up nice and she is smiling. He looks fine and straight in his suit. There's a piece of card with paintings on it, and it's of tables laid with food and animals dressed up like people.

Christmas is here, I tell Andrew.

Andrew doesn't like the treasures with animals in them dressed up foolish to look like people, but I do. I think I know what it feels like to be a mouse, small and creeping, belly to the ground.

It aint a hex. This is the thing what belongs here, in this

world. The same as mine, but whole, and mine is still where I left it. I am torn into pieces by wanting. I want to slip this whole one down my throat and fill myself with it, fill myself rounder and rounder and keep it for always. For ever always.

I wind the key and the music pours out, invisible pinpricks of sound. Downstairs, is Andrew stirring? *I can hear music, Clara.*

I put it back gently so as not to wake her. I look at her again and this time I see. I *recognize*. For everything what's broken in my world there's one what's whole here. Even girls. Even me. She *is* me, in this world, soaped glossy clean, sweet-scented and cream-skinned.

I pick up my own globe, the one what's broke. I turn the key. My tears are silver and they sting. And then wanting girdles me, I can't breathe for it. The only thing that will set my breath to rights is *thieving*—just this one thing, this one small thing in all her world of things. Surely that won't cost me extra. The medicine's for Andrew, so isn't it fair that I take something for me? When the silver door appears, I scoop up her music box, so I have what's whole and she has what's broke, and I push myself gasping through the poisonous film that separates one world from the next, and I don't feel a thing. I am glutted full.

Claire stirs and opens her eyes.

She has never seen music before, only heard it. Now, still thick with sleep, in a waking dream, she wonders at the music-box music shimmering against her open door. And she is surprised that it looks exactly as she would expect music to look. This music, anyway. Some music would look more like insects and some like clockwork and some would be deep and brown like a wood full of trees. But this music looks exactly as it should, liquid silver and iridescent, beautiful and menacing.

She sits up. The dream is fading, she remembers so little, but she knows something important has been lost, has been taken behind the silver curtain. She is seized by the knowledge that she must follow, to retrieve it. As the last note fades she stands suddenly and thrusts herself through the fading film of music, only to find herself, disappointingly, merely on the other side of her own doorway, not transported at all. She feels a sharp wrench of loss. At first she thinks it is the half-forgotten dream she mourns, but then she remembers, *Charlie.* Her eyes thick with sleep and salt, she pads down the blurred hallway, sliding her hand along the wall.

From the landing she looks down on her parents. Her mother is sitting on the floor, leaning against the front door, her head in her hands. Claire's father sits on the middle step, hunched. She can't see his face, nor hear a sound, but his shoulders jerk as they rise and fall.

She turns and runs on tiptoe back to her room. She throws herself onto the bed, burying herself under the covers, leaving only a crack through which to breathe. She squeezes her eyes closed. And: *This is the dream,* she wills desperately. *The dream girl. She is real and she has made phantoms of us all—me, Mum, Dad, Pia, Charlie.*

Suddenly the dream floods back, and she remembers it all—Clara, Andrew, Groom, Doctor, the Velvet Lady. If Claire can dream herself back there, and if Andrew can be made to live, then surely, her dream-addled brain tells her, Charlie can also live. The twin worlds will steady on their joint axis, sharing the same dream. Peacefulness will be restored.

Charlie, she thinks.

She plunges back into sleep.

The last of the music drains away. Fairyland is gone and I'm back in the broken house in the broken city, and there's a colorless sky curving over me like a great glass globe, holding the dark in. *Fairyland's what's real,* I think. *Fairyland is real, and here is what's made up.*

I peer into the wholeness of the box. As the fairyland behind me fades, it feels like this box has schemed itself into being, into wholeness. Has built itself up out of dust, from my wishes and wants. And now it's the music box what's wanting: it wants to be feasted upon. It demands me to look and look and look forever. It wants to fix me in its gaze, until I starve for everything but it. It's not gentle with its wanting. It's sharp and painful and hot, tearing at me like a rusted nail shreds at skin.

And the cruelest thing is that I will have to leave it behind. I will have to leave it here, at the edge of my world, right in the place where the door opened, because it cannot come any farther on the journey with me.

I peer down through the spaces in the floor into the murky dark. There's no solid staircase here, all fit together, all smart and clean. I have to jump, or climb, or fall—and without breaking my neck. I can't do it with a music box in my arms. What is the point of its wholeness if I break it into bits or crush it with my own self? I hover over it, then turn, hardening myself against the pain of longing. I ignore a tear that streaks down my cheek. I am cheated, rooked all over again. I want the music box. My want for it fills me to the very ends of my self. But I hate it too, I hate it with blinding white. And I am sorry for it because of how much I hate it, how much I love it.

The door to fairyland is shut fast. I place the music box careful just outside. As I place it down, a few stray notes of music tinkle out, but there aint no bubbles now, just the plinks and groans of the mechanism winding down. I hover over it for a beating of my heart, or two, then I turn away. I can have the music box and nothing. Stay up here, having the music box to the end of days. Or I can take these pills and go and save Andrew. Isn't that what the music box were for?

My arms are aching and empty, my heart awhirl. I tiptoe along the joists again; the house's skeleton cricks and cracks under the weight of me. Beneath me is darkness and shadow and gloom.

"There she is," a voice from below floats up. "About time too. Well, Salvador. Catch her. Use your girth. That's what you're for."

I peer down. It's Dolores. From up here I can see a glittering bald spot on the top of Salvador's greased-up head. His head is small but the rest of him is giant.

"Come on, Salvador. This one thing and your debt is paid in full. You can have your name back, fair and square. Consider yourself lucky."

Salvador edges on his toes, delicate despite his size. He finds a spot in the rubble under the hole in the floor. He looks up at me. I look down on him.

"Oi," he tells. "What's going on? You didn't tell me she's got the Raiders' mark. I can't do her no harm."

"I aint asked you to harm her. I asked you to catch her. It's the opposite of harm, innit?"

"'Allo, girlie," he tells up to me. "Can you fly?"

I shake my head.

"Can you fall?"

I think about it. "Yeah. I can fall." I tuck the pills into my sleeve for safety.

Salvador catches me. My jaw crunches against my chest, but nothing breaks. Salvador staggers under my weight.

"Put her down," Dolores tells. Salvador is bigger'n stronger'n Dolores, but he's feared of her, cause he does just what she tells. She puts a scrap in his paw and he clenches it. "You're paid up. Off you go. This is secret women's business here, aint it, Clara, my darlin'?"

At her bidding the giant Salvador scuttles up the shadowy street like a cockroach and I'm sorry to see him go. I aint sure why Dolores is here. Was I s'posed to bring something back for her as well? Was that our bargain? Would she send me back, through the door? And how, without Salvador there to throw me to the second story? Or was she come to take me away, to make me do some trick for her, like poor old Salvador?

"Did you get them?" Dolores asks. Her eyes glitter.

"I got 'em."

"Let me see."

What's she up to? "No."

"I gotta check 'em. See if they're the right ones."

"They were the only ones there."

"Aint gonna do your boyfriend no good if you're giving him aspirin, now, is it? He aint got toothache."

I look at her. She's waiting. She's patient. She'd wait all night. And how do I know what I got? I aint even sure what aspirin is. I hand 'em over.

She looks. "That's the ones. Well, aint you just the ticket? Didn't you turn out just right, like well-done beef? I knew it. Wobblins and tremblins. Knew you'd bring home the bacon for Miss Dolly. Mum knew too. Didn't she?"

"What?"

"It's got our name on it. See?" She points at a word on the bottle. "It's got *our* name. Jay-hay-are-vee-eye-ess. This aint for your boy. This is for Mother. Don't know what we'd do without our Mother."

She puts it deep into her cleavage. I spit. I punch at her eye. I punch for the medicine I need and also for the rage of the music box, found and lost all in one day, left behind at the door to fairyland, beyond my reach now that I'm down on the ground. I'm raged with everything Dolores has given and taken, with everything that's slipped through my fingers this night. With one hand I grab the hairs that poke out from under her brown hat and I plunge my other hand down after them pills. My fingertips close on the lid.

She laughs at me. To her I'm a flea, to be bitten away. She grabs my wrist and squeezes. I yank harder on her hair. "Now, now," she tells. "You don't think Salvador was the only one I brought with me tonight?"

Juzzy the screw steps out.

"You'd be surprised the people who owe me. Business is booming."

Juzzy takes my shoulders gently, but his fingers are firm, to let me know he's strong. I let go of her hair. She tosses her head and extracts my hand from her bosom. The pills slip away.

"You can't take 'em," I say. "I *need* 'em. Please. The music box. You can . . ." I hesitate, clenching my eyes shut. "You can have it," I spit. "I brought the Other back with me, whole and good. It must be worth something to someone, all pretty and fine. Bring back Salvador, he can throw me up there, just like he fetched me down."

Dolores laughs. "You daft child, what would I want a thing like that for? That's your treasure, not mine. Not no one else's neither. What's it worth, whole or broke, to one who can't use it?"

I spit at her.

"You got what you want, market hag," Juzzy tells. "I got work to get back to."

Dolores makes a great show of rearranging her hat, tucking in all those hairs.

"Who was the girl?" I ask. "Where you sent me? Who was she? Why did she look . . . like me?"

"You *should* ask: Who was she dreaming?"

Juzzy holds me. I can feel the warmth of his body. He won't hurt me, not with Boedica's mark still on me. But he aint gonna help neither. They're all feared of Dolores, those big men. She owns their names. Dolores tucks her last hairs away, back into her hat. "What happened to yer four-legged friend?" she asks.

I stare at her.

"Wandered off, did he? That'd be right. Oh well, duck. It'll find its way home. They always do, turning up like a bad smell." She dislodges a small piece of paper from her sleeve and drops it at my feet. "There we are, darlin'. Debt paid. In full. You can tell Juzzy how it feels. He's a long way off yet, aren't you? Poor pet." Finally she steps out onto the street. "Cheerio, little ones. It's been a pleasure doing business."

"Who was she?" I shout. "Who was the girl?"

But Dolores sticks up one hand and keeps tottering toward the shadows.

"Who was she dreaming?" I whimper, but Dolores can no longer hear.

I don't fight Juzzy. I let him hold me till she's gone. And then, when he does let go, I fall. I lie where he leaves me, for a while.

Everything's gone. At the doorway I sway, trying to see what I am seeing.

There's nothing of Andrew but his empty pile, rags fit for burning.

One thing and another, everything's falling apart, slipping away.

This is what happens when you sign your name away, Andrew in my head tells me.

Look who's talking, I tell him back. I feel round in my pocket. I realize I aint got his paper no more. I musta dropped it somewhere in the fairy place.

If there's no Andrew, it don't matter that I aint got medicine. I can sleep and this night will be over, this long and crowded, empty night. But there is an Andrew, aint there? So that means I have to go and drag my feet and find him and bring him home to live or die. And there's only one person 'sides me what cares where Andrew is, day or night. I gotta go back *there*. I gotta go back to Doctor's.

Now Groom's in my head, telling: Aint he better off there?

I ignore him. I gotta keep moving. Moving keeps me awake. I feel the dried paint of Boedica's mark on my forehead. It won't last forever, that protection, but it might take me a bit further tonight.

Groom won't shut up: Doctor's got all the medicine Andrew needs. Doctor wants what you want; he can look after Andrew. Come to me, and I will make you a nest, all feathered and soft and you can hushabye, and I'll feed you honey and sweet in the morn. I'll take care after you. I'll take care after you for only ever always.

But Doctor don't want what I want, I know. Well, he does, he wants exact same thing as me, with his own twisting.

Doctor wants to keep Andrew and build hisself a life round having him. If it's Doctor makes him well, he won't never let him go. Andrew will owe him and owe him and owe him, black and blue.

And that's why I'm in the street again, treading the same path, this night that takes me looping round and round.

It's the last time of the night when *everything* sleeps, Raiders and dogs and nightwings and all, the last time afore day. The end of night is greasy and quiet, except for my imaginings. It seems to me of a sudden that the territory of the river is growing and the city is in retreat. The river is spreading toward me, and if it takes me I'll lose myself, forget my name, forget Andrew too. It will rush over me with its wildness, it will pull me into itself. I gotta keep moving. I run and suddenly I'm sure there's dogs behind me and if I stop running they'll tear me, skin and tongue and bone.

When I get to Doctor's house, my knees give way. I crawl to the windows. There's a light in there, flickering. The party's been cleared away, there aint a body left. I can't see no Doctor, but I know he's got rooms in the back, places to keep himself and the things he wants hidden.

I slither inside and crouch, panting against the wall like the possum-rat he thinks I am.

How you gonna find him? Groom asks. How you gonna take him home?

I'm for Doctor now, Andrew tells. Save yourself, Clara.

Light crowds the corners of my eyes. Shadows enter the room and whisper. I crawl into the middle of space. I'm for Andrew and Andrew's for me. Which means if Andrew's for

Doctor then I'm for Doctor too. So I don't have to find no one, I crow to Groom. It's them that's gotta find me.

No! tells Andrew.

No! begs Groom.

But it's too late. I'm here, right where I want to be, and I'm found.

They carry me into a room and put me down on a table, two of Doctor's men and Doctor himself. Doctor's nose bulges black and blue where I kicked him, his eyes inside all that injury are black pits.

"What do you want us to do with her?" they tell.

Groom is wild in my head, howling with grief. Andrew's gone quiet. Andrew's gone still.

Doctor's voice is cold, like the river. "Give her a taste. I don't have time for her now."

Something pricks my arm. "I aint feared of bee stings," I tell them. But suddenly I am feared. It hurts. It *kills*. Panic floods through me and I knock the needle to the floor. I look down and see what's leaking out: silver, like the music-box music. Silver and poison like the bubbles. It's *in* me. I struggle to get up from the table, but they're holding me down. I force my eyes open. I fight to stay awake. My eyes meet Doctor's. He holds my gaze.

He wants to punish me.

"Give her another taste."

red sandals
sundress
sixyearsold
mama swinging curls
sun
shining footpath
red shoe red shoe waiting
hot leaves
citrus trees
bus
blurred window
street house house people dog car car dog house sky
last stop
sun
uncle charlie! hellocharliehellohello
picnic basket
footprints
sand waves
paddling
shells
long day
long beach
squinting photograph
scratchy towel
seagulls sunscreen cocacola through a straw
sundress
undress
knees waist
waving
look mum look charlie look at me
lookamesun

When the blinding white clears, when the dazzle is gone, when my blood runs from silver to red again, it aint night no more. Through the gaps in the boarded window is a sallow yellow sky.

There's a boy watching me. He's littler than a scrap, sitting on a low stool in front of the door.

"I'm Ketch," he tells. "I gotta watch you. Doctor give it me for my job."

I reach up to touch the paint on my forehead.

"It's gone," Ketch tells. "Doctor made us rub it away. *She* don't hold sway here. Under his roof under his rules, you are."

"And what are his rules?"

"First things first." Ketch points to a bucket of water in the corner, and a pile of cloths, and on top of that, a squared-off lump of soap. "He wants you clean."

Ketch don't want to watch me in the rawbones, I can see that right enough. But he is too feared of Doctor to look away, even when I ask in my most polite milktongue, like Boedica taught me. "You might eat soap and die," he tells me. "You might drown in the water tub." As if he'd quite like to nibble the soap or drown.

"I didn't come here to drown," I say. "I came here for Andrew. Where is he?"

"I like Andrew. He always looked after me."

"Will you take me to him?" I ask. "Will you help us?"

Ketch shakes his head. "I aint brave. That's why Doctor likes me. I always do the things what I'm told."

"What if *I* tell you to do it? Then will you?"

Ketch thinks about it. He shakes his head. "The things what Doctor tells me to do overcounts you."

"Well, I aint washing unless you watch the wall, not me. And if I don't wash, I'll be for it and I don't care. But you'll be for it too. Didn't he tell you I had to be clean?"

Ketch turns his back and watches the wall, and I see I have some sway after all, he just needs stern talk, not politeness. I strip off and stick my head in the bucket. I clean myself all over, with soap and all. For now, I think, better to follow Doctor's rules if I want to see Andrew and if I want Doctor to keep me too, at least till Andrew's better and we can run away together. There's a nice-sized rag for drying myself on and clean pants and a colored shirt with buttons. The top is tight under my arms and the pants are too short, but other than that they fit okay.

When I'm finished I go back to the table. I sit down to wait. It's a long time waiting and the torn piece of sky that I can glimpse through the window boards goes from dog-tooth yellow to dirty white. There's noises outside, metal clanking on metal, doors opening and closing, and sometimes voices, but I can't hear what they're telling. I feel slithering soap in the dips between my fingers.

"He's forgotten us," I say. Ketch is drifting in and out on his hard stool.

"He may have forgotten me," Ketch tells. He makes a rusty sound that I realize is a laugh. He aint a well thing, that boy, for all that he lives with a Doctor. "That 'appens more times than not. But he aint forgotten you."

"As long as he's making Andrew well." After a bit I add, "Can't you breathe quieter?"

Ketch tries to obey, but all he manages is long pauses between noisy, ragged breath.

"Ketch, I can't sit no more. Isn't there some way of making him come?"

The breath-holding has worn him out. He's gone to sleep folded over on himself. I go to the door and try the handle. It won't turn. I rattle the door. I press my ear on the wood. I can't hear nothing now. No clanking. No voices rumbling. Not a whisper. Not a squeak.

I lie down on the table. I stare at the ceiling. I wait.

I open my eyes. Ketch is gone. I stand and pad to the door. This time the handle turns. I peer out the room. Aint no one there waiting for me. I walk as fast as I can, but I don't bother hiding. I find another door and then another. I look in each one.

In the last room laid out on a table is Andrew. There's a jar on a stand above his head, and what looks like blood inside. There's a thin bit of clear piping traveling down from the jar and into Andrew.

That's not me, Andrew in my head tells.

Oh you're back, are you?

But he's right. That aint Andrew. It's something Doctor made, like he took himself a dead thing and tried to make it live.

This is your chance, Clara, Andrew tells. Run.

I gotta stay here, I tell Andrew. If I go, I've lost you.

You've already lost me. That thing of bone and skin is ragging its last breaths. Life is already gone. The body needs to catch up, that's all.

I clench my teeth. Then if you're gone, I may as well be here as anywhere.

Oh, Clara, Andrew tells, don't say that. And it is so exactly his voice that I can't bear it. I go back to my prison, pull the door closed, and wait.

Next time I open my eyes Ketch is back, sitting on his stool, but this time pulled up close to the table. He don't look so ill now. "Things is different," he tells.

"Different how?"

"There's new rules" is all he will say.

"What rules?"

He won't tell. "We gotta wait," he tells. "We gotta wait and see."

"Is there anything to eat?" I ask. "I'm starving."

He gives me something from his pocket that feels hard as stone, but I discover when I scrape my teeth along it that it's bread. I work away at it for a time.

"What are we waiting for?"

Ketch don't answer. Instead he whispers, "He knows how to hurt a body. He knows how to hurt you so you stay hurt. You shoulda scarpered when you had the chance."

So it was Ketch who left the door cracked open. "Why do *you* stay?" I ask.

Ketch looks surprised. "Where else would I go? Where would I find another what loves me and looks after me like he does?"

"Them that love you don't hurt you."

Ketch thinks about that. "I aint never been hurt by someone I didn't love."

That's all we have to say to each other. We go back to waiting.

I'm blurring in and out of being awake again when the door crashes open. I sit up gasping. So does Ketch.

I slither off the table and stand to face him. Doctor reaches me in two steps and puts a hand at my throat. He aint used to doing his own violence, I can tell. He'd usually get his men to do it. He acts his violence on a body once it's already laid down. But he catches me surprised and up against the wall I go, twitching like a bug. He's fat more'n muscle, but he lifts me all the same, and I know it's his feelings what are powerful, not his beef.

We're face to face. We're eye to eye. His face is swollen,

still blue and black where I kicked him. I can't breathe, but it don't matter up here, does it? I'm looking in his eye and he's looking in mine until he's sure I know what he knows.

Andrew is dead. That body, that thing laid up. Is dead.

Then he drops me on the floor to cower. I don't want to give him no satisfaction, but I can't raise my head. I'm ready for the silver, for another taste. I'm ready for him to fill me so full of it I go where Andrew's gone, cause what's the point of anything without him? Why drag this cruel world into my lungs, this bitter scent? Why breathe a day in and a day out, when all them days are lined up, row upon row, all empty of him?

"Get up, market scum," Doctor tells.

I get up. Ketch is cradling his head. He won't look. He won't even look. Coward.

I want Doctor to hurt me so it don't stop. I want to be hurt. I'm no coward. I won't flinch. And he rages at me, I can see it under his skin, the violence brewing—he wants to tear me bone from bone. But instead two men come in and afore I can see what's going on, there's some kind of sacking on my head. It smells vegetable.

Doctor squeezes my arm and growls into my ear. "I won, though, didn't I, filthtramp? He was mine in the end. He never was more mine than laid out on that table, filling up with Ketch's blood." No wonder Ketch had looked so feeble, with his blood drained out. Had Doctor wanted me to see Andrew like that? Is that why Ketch had left the door acrack? Ketch were a coward, he said so himself. He only did what Doctor told him.

"Here now," another voice tells. "Don't bruise the fruit." I thought this bag was on my head for more violence, or for being drowned in the river, like a clutch of puppies. But no. I am being exchanged like a market good.

"Take it away. Tell your Boss if it comes near me again I will squash it like the filthy cockroach that it is."

Doctor leaves. I can feel he is gone though I can't see, I can feel the grief and rage he is dragging being sucked out of the room. They tie my hands behind my back.

"Where are you taking me?"

No one answers.

"Ketch? You here?" But if he is, his lips are clammed, his head is cradled, he's gone into himself like one of them gray beetles I used to play with, balling 'em up and rolling 'em along the ground. "Bye, Ketch," I say.

I wish you were brave, Ketch. I wish you could go to market and get Groom and tell him to come find me, Ketch. I wish your blood were stronger, Ketch. I wish it had been brave blood, and had gone in fighting.

And now I am a parcel, a thing what belongs to someone, what's been swapped by Doctor. And it don't matter who's done the swapping because I am owned, just like I was afore, when Dolores had my name. I only had it back for a little while and I was so frantic looking for Andrew that I had no time to enjoy belonging to myself again, and then I was Doctor's, and now whose I am is a mystery, but I'm not my own something no more.

Andrew, I tell solemn. You was right and I was wrong. I should never have signed my name away. But Andrew aint there no more. And it's a great shame cause he would have liked being right.

And then I am stung with sadness and under this bag aint no one to see the tears that roll, so I let 'em, one after another dripping into my mouth. But they know I am grieving just the same because I am dragged and pushed and pulled and carried; to remind me to be a parcel and not a girl, not a living breathing feeling thing.

I'm delivered on my knees. I kneel, still tethered and bagged. Someone unties me, delicately picking at the knots instead of cutting the rope. When my hands are free, I pull the bag off and blink in the dazzling light.

It's her, the Velvet Lady, the Lady Boedica, kneeling in front of me.

She does not speak. She takes a cloth and wets it in warm, perfumed water and dabs away the tears.

"You can cry, my own one," she tells. "You can cry as much as you like. I'm for you now. I bargained and I won you, my sweet child, fair and square."

It's her giving me let to cry that dries up my tears once and for all.

"How did you know I was at Doctor's?"

"I have a little sparrow installed under Horace's care. He twitters and tweets and tells me all sorts of shining things." Ketch? Maybe. After all, he aint brave and it don't seem a very brave thing, to be a twitterer. "And so I sent my emissary to make terms."

"What terms?"

"You needn't worry yourself with the contract. You're here

for good. He can't take you back. Not without War, and there's no one wants War. Peace is fragile and violent, but War is worse."

I ask again. "What terms?"

She gives one last furious rub on my cheek with her wet cloth. "If Andrew died, you lived and I could have you."

"And if Andrew lived?"

"Well, it didn't come to that, now, did it?" She rubs my hair between her fingers, then leans closer and sniffs it. "You've washed your hair."

"He woulda killed me," I say. "Either way, he made sure Andrew would never be mine."

"Andrew was his favorite," Boedica tells, like it's the only fact what counts. She combs her fingers through my hair, tugging the ends gently into place. "Andrew was Horace's best boy."

I pull away. She folds her cloth and picks up her water dish. *Andrew is mine,* I whisper to myself. *He is my Favorite. He is my Best.*

"You stay here and rest. Brown and Duguld are outside if you want for anything."

What things would I want for now?

It don't take long for me to know that Boedica's is also a prison. Brown and Duguld get me anything I ask for and things I don't: oranges and creamy white drinking peppermint and words to read and a long dark dress, hot soup for sipping, cushions for sleeping, oh, all very fine. The room she keeps me in is large, with places to sit and places to lie and places for thinking, and even a window looking out at a wall no matter which way you crane your head, but letting light in just the same. It don't look like a trap for a greasemouse at all, but that is what it is. And a greasemouse trapped is what I am.

Boedica tells I don't have to work for her. I am hers and she will keep me. A frightening numbness swells in me. I cram apples and oranges and drinking peppermint into the empty, unfeeling places. I lie on cushions and sleep. I count all the things I've lost over and over again: Andrew and dog and Groom and even the dreaming girl in fairyland. I think about the music box, whole and perfect and abandoned, and how tight its own longing must be. I count the antibiotics and my crumbles for taking apart and fixing and market and my name and after a while also Dolores and her mother and Pip and Ketch, the river dog, and, yes, even Doctor. I hoard 'em inside me, I won't let any of 'em slip away.

So a loop of days goes by: Duguld and Brown and others watching over, Boedica to come and go, all of 'em fetching and carrying after me. And after a while I find out I can have anything I tell 'em, but nothing that I want—the things she can't give me, like Andrew and dog and Groom and the life I had once. This is what Ketch meant. This is why Doctor gave me away. He knew how to hurt me so I'd keep on hurting: red and black and blue.

One day Boedica comes. Something is bundled in her arms; at first I think it's a pup. I can't see it, I can just hear its snuffles.

"It's a baby," she laughs, taking pleasure in my mistake. "You ever held a baby?"

I shake my head. There's babies at market of course, but they all belong to someone. She bundles it into my arms afore I can say if I want it.

"Hello, baby," I say. I don't mind it. Its big blue-gray eyes are open wide, but it don't see me. It's looking at window-light.

"Silly, it doesn't know one thing from another yet. It doesn't know hello or goodbye."

Lucky baby. But then I think: it knows light from shadow.

I pile the baby and blankets back in her arms. She watches it hungrily for a while. It begins to cry and fuss.

"Hush," she tells fiercely, shaking the little pile. "Hush." When the baby don't hush she puts it on the floor, not gently. She walks over to the frosted window.

"I know!" She claps. "Would you like to come out for a walk?"

"Outside? Now?"

"Oh, come now, Clara," she tells, and she reminds me of me: pestering for Andrew to take me to market or read stories with me.

I think on it and nod. I am sick of inside, of stale air.

"What about the baby?"

She glances at it, as if surprised it is still here. It's sending itself off to sleep, never mind the cold hard floor under its tiny skull. "Someone will fetch it," she tells.

I feel a stirring anxiety for the poor grub, all wrapped up tight against air and bugs but defenseless all the same.

I eye Boedica, wondering at the jagged edges of her, the part of her that *wants* and the part of her that discards as easily. I think that she would leave me one day in a place cold and hard, but the thought is thin and don't last. I don't care enough, about being wanted or being left. Even when it comes to the baby, most of what I am is numb. I follow her out the door.

Brown and Duguld join us. They stroll along behind us, as if they were just taking in sights. I wonder if Boedica's worried I might run. She tells it is just a jaunt we are on, but I see she means to show me the fortifications. We are inside a city block, she tells. *Right inside!* And all the houses is built together to make for strong walls. Aint no one getting in unless they're let. Aint no one getting out either, is what she doesn't say. As if I had the energy, or the will, to run. As if I had somewhere to take myself.

Boedica leads me through her place. It don't look like a fortification. It looks like a market. There's tents and tables everywhere, but they aint selling. They're *living.* Talking and laughing and squabbling. One old man throws a bone at a woman's head and three others descend and take her by the shoulders and cluck and tattle. There's a whole family together, a man stirring a pot over a fire and a woman throwing slippery meat into it, and children playing. There's dogs lying round, being thrown scraps of fat or having their bellies scratched. Mostly people are all right, though I see the women stare warily at us as we walk past, and menfolk call their children softly to their sides. All I know of Raiders is hunting and drinking and fighting. I never thought they'd have children, and laughing.

A man is holding a woman, and she is wringing her hands till the blood inside them turns blue. She wrenches away and clasps Boedica's dress sleeve.

"Oh, Lady, begging pardon, where's my baby?"

Boedica stares down her long nose. I wonder if she even remembers the infant she left dozing on the stone floor. "Do you love me?" she asks the grieving mother finally.

The mother grips the sleeve. "Yes, Lady."

"Does your baby love me?"

"Oh yes, Lady." Tears stream down her cheeks.

As if business is done here, Boedica makes to walk on. The mother doesn't release the sleeve though.

"Only, Lady, it's past feeding and I ache for him."

Boedica looks at me and then at her. She laughs a little, but fury ripples under her skin—she reminds me of Doctor. "It's good for us to ache, isn't it, Clara? Aching makes us strong."

I glance from Lady to mother and bite my tongue.

"Now tell my new pet girl how happy we are here."

"Oh yes," the mother tells miserably. "Ever so."

The wretched mother moves back to her man, who clutches her hard enough that it looks painful.

That's when I see Ole John. The screws is paid for by Bosses, so I guess it aint impossible that he's a Raider as well as a screw, but I am jibbered to see him here. If he knows who I am he don't show it. He sees me and looks away. I think those two girls with orange hair must be his daughters. They're stitching. One of them, young like me, is making cheer, but the older one is scowling and keeps sticking herself with the pin. The scowling one catches me staring and sticks her tongue out like a child, though she'd be Groom's age and not less.

Maybe it aint a prison after all, is what Boedica's showing me, if there's food, and round cooking pots, and fathers with daughters who prick themselves with pins, and babies in bundles, and well-kept dogs. Maybe it's a place for a girl like me, who aint got a one of my own, who aint got nowhere better to go.

When we get back the baby is gone. There's a gleaming thread of goldy hair, and a leftover smell of milky soursweet. That's all.

This is how I live: I wake each new morning to a breakfast tray, sometimes lemons cut thin and sprinkled with salt, sometimes a bowl of freshly curdled milk, sometimes gravy pie. I wash a little (but I don't take soap). I sit at the window and make words with my readings until Boedica or Duguld or Brown takes me outside. In the evenings, there's another meal: bread and honey soaked in milk, or birds' eggs in soup, or thin fried meat and grated fruit. There's company if I want. Most times I'm alone.

Days fall in together and I don't miss one after it's gone.

There's things left in the world to wonder about, like Groom and dog and my old squat where I lived with Andrew, but all of 'em belong to another girl, one no more like me than the dreamer in fairyland. My grief for Andrew mixes with my grief for Groom, like he's dead too. I know he must think I am.

I aint any closer to figuring why Boedica won me from Doctor, and if she got plans for me besides feeding me sweet and keeping me locked, though I don't spare much time wondering about it. I know she don't trust me yet, don't believe I'm fixing to stay, because she keeps me guarded. And maybe I'm not, but I aint fixing to go nowhere neither. There's a life I lived once that was made bearable by having Andrew to share it with. I could leave here and things could be better or they could be worse, without salted lemons or bread in milk. For every Groom out there there's a Pip, waiting to take a hair, and other things besides. So I'm staying for now, like a snail coiled inside his shell, like a slaty beetle, all curled up inside myself.

That's how I am when the earthquake comes.

That's how Andrew calls it when he whispers in my ear: Wake up, Clara. Wake up. An earthquake is here. I wake up with tears rolling down my cheeks though I don't remember no dreams.

There's rumblings, deep and powerful. I go out to the vestibule, looking for Brown or Duguld. They are both there tonight sitting on the floor, backs against the stone wall, listening.

"What's happening?" I ask. I aint feared, just wondering. "What's that noise?"

"It's quaking, it's shaking, she's waking," Duguld tells. His eyes are bright. They been passing a bottle between them.

"Who's waking? Boedica?"

"Almost up for you, little shadow," Brown tells. "Boedica's almost won you, only ever always."

"I thought she already won me. From Doctor."

"Though why she would want you aint a tale worth telling," Duguld tells, as if I hadn't said nothing.

"Is it War?" I ask.

Duguld seems to find this amusing, and he giggles high-pitched, like a child.

"Go back to bed," Brown tells. "Go back to bed and see if you're still here in the morning."

Outside the garbage truck clanks and groans, rumbling down the street. Morning is arriving, spreading over the sky like a broken egg. You could wake now, you think, somewhere inside dreaming.

You know, without opening your eyes, that there is a dark shape in your room, a large presence heavy with sadness, you can feel the weight of it on the air. This shape breathes. It is Pia. She sits on the bed watching you sleep, and the mattress creaks. Her hand reaches for your forehead, but before her fingers touch your skin, she hesitates and pulls her hand away. She rises, her movements slow with the child she carries in the deep of her flesh. She departs, sorrow billowing behind her, leaving the shadow of her in the room, leaving the outline of emptiness. Perhaps all this is a dream too.

You could wake now, but you won't. Not yet. Not yet.

In the morning, before I open my eyes, I breathe the vapors of smoky cabbage potch and I know I'm still here. I go out to tell them, Brown and Duguld, but it is them that are gone. I eat my smoky cabbage and the taste stays in my mouth. I wash it down with my goblet. I fetch my pencil stub and leaf and make my alphabets. But the emptiness of the space outside the door distracts me. I let paperleaf drift to the floor and dream instead.

Someone does come to fetch me to take me for my walk. It's Ole John.

"Hello, Miss," he tells. "Keep your head." And he leads me out. I pretend not to know him and I can tell this pleases him.

Everything looks like a regular day, no War or earthquakes here. The family's there with the little round children. The baby kicks off its blankets in its basket and is scolded by its mother, the dogs lounge and whimper. There's birds in cages. In the scraps, I see a hen peck a mouse, toss it up and choke it whole down its throat. There's Raiders with dogs getting ready to go out raiding, business as usual.

Ole John takes me to the back of his own tent. He don't look round or nothing, he holds open a flap and pushes me in. It's the orange-haired daughters I expect to see. I always look for them when I am out, one always sweet, the other always sour. But there aint no girls. I'm staring at Groom in the tentlight, and Groom's staring back at me. I can't believe I am seeing him and that he is real, nor that he is seeing me, looking me over with all his eyes, as if he can't get that I'm real neither.

"You seen her," Ole John tells. "You seen her now. That's an end to it."

"Clara," Groom tells. "I thought you was gone. I asked all over. I even went to Doctor's digs, and found a squeal called Ketch who said Andrew was dead and you'd been sold away for meat. If it weren't for Ole John I aint never of found you."

"Don't say it out loud," groans Ole John. "I got daughters worth more than you two and me put together." I see through another crack in the tent walls that his daughters is out the front, doing their stitchings, keeping lookout. "You seen her now, safe and well," Ole John tells Groom. "It's over and done."

"Are you well, Clara? Are you safe?"

I snort. "Safer than I ever been. I never thought to being this safe."

"Will you come away with me?"

Ole John groans again. "You can't," he tells. "She likes you too much. You're her thing now. You wouldn't be let."

"He's right," I tell Groom. "She means to keep me. I can't figure why, but she wants me to be hers."

"Good girl," Ole John tells. "That's keeping your head. It's politic. Our Lady's made a contract with Doctor. She's won the lass fair and square. She can't grant right nor freedom or they'd call weak after her and make War."

"Aint no one ever put Clara in a pocket. Even Andrew let you come and go how you pleased. What's happened to you, Clara?"

I stick my chin out. "I grew up. I had to."

"She has grown," Ole John tells. "Look at her."

"You grew feared," spits Groom.

"I gotta take her back now," Ole John clucks. "You seen her. It's done."

"Wait." Groom reaches for me and my heart turns over. I want him to. I want him to take me by the hand and pull me over Boedica's walls, but I know it would be death to him if I let him take me.

"There's nowhere for us," I say, this time soft. "No market or zone or lair that is out of reach of her. Don't you see?"

Ole John rocks and groans.

"There's the river," Groom tells. "There's what's on the other side."

"Aint no one crossed the river!" chides Ole John. "No, she stays here where it's safe, where if she never makes trouble it's safe for all her days."

"That don't sound safe," Groom tells. "You tellin me

Boedica won't grow tired of her? You tellin me Boedica won't do her no harm?"

"You're the one wants her to cross the river."

Groom wheels on me. "You think you're the only girl Boedica's collected this way? You think you're special? She could have hundreds in there, in all them fortified rooms."

I step away, and I'm stung. It never occurred to me to think that there might be girls and girls, rooms of them, eating their sweets, brushing their hairs, receiving their attentions from Boedica.

Ole John takes my arm.

"I'll wait for you," Groom tells. "I'll wait for you outside the walls."

"They'll find you!"

"They'll gut you." Ole John's words is flat, matter-of-fact.

"It can't be worse than feelin this," Groom tells. "I don't care if they kill me."

"*I* care," I say. And I do. Unexpected care fills me, bruising my eyes with tears.

"Do you?" Groom asks. "All this time I never knew. Do you?"

I clamp my mouth. Maybe if he thinks I don't care he'll go back to market, back to his silver girl. He'll be forgetting me and that's the way Groom lives, even if I am stuck here forever, for the end of my days. The numbness that's been whorling in me all these long Boedica days is breaking apart, and another darkness is setting in, a grief so painful and raw that I almost can't bear it.

I always cared, I want to tell him. *I always split my heart between Andrew and you. Just that, till now, Andrew got the bigger piece. But now Andrew's gone. . . .* I stop my tongue. If I tell these things, Groom will risk all for me, and it's too much.

"The sooner you come, the less I'll be killed," he tells me. "If you care, you'll care about that."

"That aint fair!"

"Caged birds don't sing, Clara."

"But you just want to put me in another kind of cage."

"I won't wait too long," Groom promises. "Not more'n three days. You know I can hide myself that long. If you don't come, then I'll disappear, back to market for good. That's fair."

"This aint the kinda trouble I invited," frets Ole John, jangling a ring of keys. I wonder which is the one that would open the door to let me have my freedom with Groom. "I have to take her back."

I look at Groom's mouth when I say goodbye, not at his river-brown eyes, for fear of drowning in them. I won't make no vows.

Ole John leads me on a hasty circuit, so all can claim to have seen me, and then back to my room. Duguld is back, dozing in the vestibule. Ole John leaves me there without a word, but the last grip of his hand on my arm tells me what he's thinking right enough, and later, when he's gone, there's a bruise the size of his thumb to remember by.

I lean against the wall and touch my lips with my fingers. Ole John is right, I can't go. "Goodbye, Groom," I say. "Goodbye."

That night supper is a pot of soupy rice with sweet peppers, and a ladle and two bowls. The Lady Boedica comes to me. "Are you happy here, Clara?" she asks me as we chase the last grains round the edges of our bowls.

I eye her warily. "I aint always *un*happy." I put my bowl down. "Are you happy, Lady?"

She laughs. "Oh, you are such a treat, my girl. What can I bring you to make you happier? More books, a songbird in a cage, a puppy? Oh yes, a puppy!"

I shake my head. "I got a dog."

"You *had* a dog," Boedica snaps. "Why do you make it so hard to love you?" She turns to look at the last of the light filtering in between the wall and the window glass. "I could move you," she tells suddenly. "You could have a room with a view, right over the Raiders' town. Then you would feel a part of things, all the time."

I shrug. Ever since Groom, the thought has been chipping at me, what is it Boedica wants from me? Is he right? Has she a jumble of girls pigeoned away, room on room on room?

Her eyes glitter, annoyed. "Let me love you. Just name the things that you want."

I thought wanting had gone stale in me, that there weren't things to want no more. But not so. Seeing Groom has loosened the wanting in me, and my tongue prattles: "I'd like to go to market sometimes, just to look, not to buy. I'd like to see my old digs, what I shared with Andrew. And I'd like to take some food to Ketch, you have plenty and he's so little and thin, and maybe with a full-up belly he could learn to be brave. I'd like . . . I want . . ." I don't know how to ask for Groom, because he aint a thing she can give me. And if he were then he would be prisoner here too. Thinking of Groom being kept inside these walls makes me realize, sharp-breathed, how trapped I really am, how much of myself I have lost in losing my free wanderings, the city I owned once afore, the places I was boss of myself.

Anyways, the way her face is setting, I know that I have already pushed my luck too far.

Too late I think, *I should have asked for the music box.* She'd of got me that. It's the kind of thing she wants me to want—something to fix me in place, to hold me in the hexery of wanting.

She snatches my bowl from the floor, clatters the pots back onto the tray. "Clara, you ask too much. You are always asking for too much, even when you're not asking for anything. You want to eat this world whole like an apple, and then you'd just ask for more." Boedica stands up and pulls me roughly to my feet. "Come with me. I do have something for you." Her lip curls up. "A gift."

She holds my hand in hers so squeezingly I think my bones will be crushed. She strides through the corridors, from one joined-up house to the next. I can barely keep up. I can feel anger and strength in her and I know if I stumble she will drag me, as if I am no weight at all. She takes me down a flight of sharp steps, into the creeping cold. She stops at a large metal door.

"I caught something this morning. We've been looking for

it a while now, it was garnering too much power. I thought you might like to play with it before we dispose of it."

She draws a long bony key from her sleeve and slides it stiffly in the lock. The door swings open and she pushes me ahead of her.

I smell meat.

In the center of the stone room—stone walls, stone floor—tied to a chair, her arms bound to her side, her mouth gagged, is Dolores. She makes a low growl in her throat when she sees Boedica, but I can see she's feared. Her puffed up fleshiness is sagging all over. Her eyes are bright and black. Her hair is no longer pinned inside her hat, but streaking down on her face, thick with blood.

Boedica strides to the chair. She looms over Dolores. "Now, now," she tells. "You keep a clean tongue. There are children present." She pulls down the gag. Dolores immediately peals off language to skin a cat and Boedica laughs. She turns to me. "I know the two of you are old friends, so I will let you catch up."

"That aint necessary." I take her hand.

"But I insist." Boedica smiles grimly, shaking me off like she would a greasemouse, and I know I'm being punished for something. For not letting her love me. As the metal door swings closed, I gasp for air. It's foul in here. It smells worse than meat. It smells like death.

"What sort of trouble you got yourself into now?" Dolores tells.

I eye her. Even though she's trussed up wing and leg like one of Boedica's eating hens, I don't trust her.

Me being wary pleases her no end. "That's right, you watch

for me. I got myself out of worse scrapes than this. I still got ones what owe me, even under her roof." She peers critically at me through her swollen eyes. "It's you what's lost and can't be found."

"Because of you! I was all right afore you come along with your rooking and that cursed box. I was for Andrew and Andrew was for me."

"Because of me? Ungrateful. I gave you everything you wanted. I exhausted myself giving to you." She is just like Boedica. Dolores keeps tattling. "And look where it got me. All my life I've lived for others, never claiming nothing for my own. . . ."

"You! With your fistful of names! Owning all them souls."

"And none of them came but willingly. And who are you to talk? You with your reckless wanting, cracking the world apart!"

I scowl. "I never wanted nothing. Just to keep what was mine."

Dolores laughs, liquid burbling in her throat. "Oh, not asking for much, is she? Just the sun and the moon and the stars. That's all! Just the world to rust on its axis, that's all."

"It weren't nothing," I say. "Just Andrew and Groom. Just to wear my groove between market and home, and to quarry and to mend, to live as we live, that's all."

"That's all. That's all." She lolls in her chair, catching her breath. I walk the walls, looking for some trickery, some hidden handle or key, that will let me out of here and away from her ramblings. Dolores is fading, but her eyes are merciless bright. "Listen. You stay here with the Lady. You stay here with her always and she will love you, eat you, sell you, keep you, hate you, forget you all at the same time. She likes what's precious, adorns her little palace with precious things, don't she? Until the shine rubs off."

"I aint precious. Why'd she pick me?"

Dolores talks to the floor. Her body is expiring, but her tongue flaps in her head as ever. "Aint she a collector? Aint she and you the same? Digging through the city for ones what others might want, seeing value in trash, looking inside them broken things and seeing a shining promise? You get that, girl? You're a crankshank for an electric clock to her."

I think on that. I aint nothing so useful to Boedica as a crankshank. If I were useful, she woulda *used* me by now. I'm a musical globe, an ornament, a bauble. Something to look at, to want, to dangle and keep. But to forget, yes. To get lost in the clutter of all her shining things. I'm special, but I aint more special than all the many special things. I'm a thing of uncertain value, worth only what she thinks I'm worth.

"Want me to loose those ties?" I watch Dolores's face leach from purple to pale. I walk over and start to jiggle the knots. If I'm trapped in here with her I can't have Dolores step out on me, slip down the black river of dreamless, after where Andrew's gone, leaving behind only the thing.

Dolores don't hear nothing but the loose bolts rattling in her brain. "But you got *her* number. You're playing the Lady's game. The longer you stay here, meek and mouse, the more she will forget you. She *wants* you to run. She wants her dogs to fetch you back by the throat. She's dying to see your colors. But look at you, fading away into nothing. That's the ticket. That's the trick. You just vanish here, little miss. You just steal your worth from under her very eyes."

Dolores is right. I can actually *feel* myself being forgotten, left down here to rot like her, I can feel the color draining outta me. I pound on the door and shout at the metal, which absorbs all sound.

And she comes for me, my Lady, by and by, and her men Brown and Duguld too. She gags Dolores, who is dead or sleeping, and takes me back upstairs, Lady in front and Brown and Duguld behind. We walk past a door just cracking open and I catch a breath, not of Raiders' Town—which is people and dog and fowl, what they eat, what they excrete—but the sulfur breath of the far-off river.

Run, tells Andrew.

Run, tells Groom. Now's your chance.

I'm out the door and I'm running, even though I know this is what Boedica wants me to do, or why else would that door be jarring open? Dolores cackles in my head, and I'm her thing too. It's Dolores what put this thought in my head, for her own mystery purpose. Dolores wants me to skedaddle.

I'm running, but I can't outrun Boedica, I can't outrun Dolores; my legs are heavy and stupid and slow. I keep moving, even when I hear dogs at my ankles, even when I hear the shouts of Raiders. Even when they corner me, and I'm surrounded by them and their long-toothed slavering dogs, my heart runs ahead. I look at the sky. I look at the city. I look to the river. From the corner of my eye I think

I see Groom, flickering from one building to the next, in the long last light of the dying day. I howl inside for everything, but mostly for Andrew and Groom and for my own dog, lost in the dreaming place, and for me, poor me, in the prison of my own self that I made with my own hands, as good and strong as Boedica done.

And I think I want to break it apart now. I want to crumble it away and to feel sky.

No cry passes my lips. I stand in the center of the Raiders, panting, facedown, as if I'm beaten, but through my lashes I gaze from one to the other. I feel something in me stretch, something wild that's been sleeping.

Boedica parts the circle of Raiders. The dogs lay down at command, to show their respect. Boedica puts her hand to my throat and tenderly squeezes until my breath chokes inside me. She smiles with the pride of a mother.

"That's it, my girl. Run run run."

I try to break free of her grip, but she holds me all the tighter.

"All I ask, Clara, my belle," she murmurs, "all I ask is that you fear me." She kisses my forehead, one burning kiss, right where her mark used to be. "Fear me and I will love you and care for you all your days and bring you wine and sweet and treasures to occupy you by."

She drops me, and I take breaths, but they taste as sour as sick.

Boedica's prison is not made of stone walls or rooms or fortifications, but of her *want*. There is no escaping, unless she desires me to, in order to make a sport of catching me and hauling me back. I glance toward the creeping river territories and I curse Groom for finding me. Since he has been here, I have *felt:* the closeness of walls, the grief of loss, the flicker of hope—blasted hope—and something warmer and deeper and more mysterious than hope. I curse Dolores for showing me how complete my prison has become. In fact, it is Dolores who has finished it off, once and for good. *And she will love you, eat you, sell you, keep you, hate you, forget you all at the same time.* Boedica's fierce kiss brands my skin and a new feeling burns me.

Fear.

In the morning Ole John's merry daughter is watching me. Her name's Aily, she tells.

"Lady sent me to keep an eye on things. Someone let Lady's marketeer go."

"Dolores?"

"It's a scandal."

I almost laugh. Dolores is an inspiration.

"It's not so funny, Miss," Aily tells. "Lady's in a right red rage. Now, I boiled us some grains, and Lady sent along butter and sweet. There's roasted apple too. You are a lucky pet."

I'm being treated special, rewarded for the fear Boedica saw flash in my eyes. I stare numbly at the wall behind Aily. "I aint hungry."

Aily spoons a bowlful for me anyway and one for herself.

"Dad says we always got to be thankful for what we get," she tells. "Cause we don't know what's coming next." She shovels in a mouthful. "You still thinking about leaving?"

I'm watchful. "I aint decided yet."

"Lady's not done you harm. Your prison's more comfortable than most lives."

"Groom tells caged birds don't sing."

"Why, that's not true." Aily's face is all smiles and bright. "We used to have one and she sang her throat pure and golden every day. And if you opened the door she never flew anywhere, she just stayed on her perch and sang." She lifts a roast apple onto her spoon and nibbles at the skin. "Are you gonna eat? It's good."

I cut some butter onto my swollen grains and sit back to watch it ooze. "What happened to it?" I ask Aily.

"What happened to what?"

"That songing bird."

"Oh, well, it died. Greya—my sister—went out to feed it and it was lying on its back and its legs were stiff and curling. That's what she said. I wouldn't look. Greya knows I don't have the stomach for dead things, but Greya said Birdie looked peaceful enough, like she were thinking up a new song."

I wonder if there's a girl on the other side of the door for Aily, just like there were for me. Some sleeping girl with her face, and one for Greya, and one for Boedica too. A music box whole for every music box what's broke in this world. Airy confections, made of sweet and salt, light and dark.

If I were a dream, I'd just sit here in Boedica's palace until I disappeared, like Dolores tells, fading away into nothing. Cause dreams don't matter. Dreams don't last.

Of course they matter, Andrew tells. Even if they don't last.

Groom tells: Sometimes they last.

I aint listening to the two of you.

I aint clever-clever like Dolores or Duguld and Brown, or seeing like Dolores's old mum. But there is one thing I do know, tucked away inside myself: hope unstitches you. Hope leaves you open and wounded. Without hope there is no fear, there is just living. Haven't I learned this very lesson all my life, by not messing with the way things are, by staying close to Andrew and living the same life every day? Aint I an expert at burying hope—gray and greasy and pulsing—under dirt, under stones? Aint I always buried it, every time Groom came calling, wanting us to make a life, we two? Aint I an age-old expert at stopping the flow of feeling, staunching the blood-river of hope and love that threatens to sweep a soul away?

"Are you gonna eat that apple?" Aily hungrily gobbles down her grain.

That was the life I was living. Saying no all the time to Groom and his fancy futures, spun from dreams. If *I* were a dream I'd just sit here. I'd staunch the blood-river forever and sit in the dim and the quiet, feeling nothing at all, fading into gray, until, forgotten, I slipped from the world altogether.

Outside, the morning is progressing. The sun creeps across your bed. Your parents mutter on the other side of the closed door.

"I'm going to wake her," Dad says.

Not yet. You squeeze your eyes shut. *It's too soon.*

"No," Mum urges. "Let her sleep."

Climbing the stairs are the steady, dogged tones of an arpeggio. There is no magic in the relentless rise and fall of these broken chords. This is earth music, hard music, the most grounded music there is. It marches into your dreaming, and though you try to hold on to the dream, you can't.

You are awake.

It is Pia at the piano. It is Pia's sadness that has woken you.

You reach out for your music box, to wind it up and hold it

to your chest and feel it strum inside you. And your fingers meet the jagged edge of glass. The dream comes back in a rush and, your eyes still closed, you see: in place of your music box, the dream interloper has left this one, a changeling of a music box, ugly and twisted, deformed and fragmented.

You sit up and take it in your arms. The bride and her mouse groom have broken apart, the groom is gone. The bride's arms hold emptiness, and her face is—to you—perceptibly sadder without him. It is made of all the wrongness of the world, this music box, every harm and sorrow. It fills you with deep shame, why you do not know, for it is not your fault it is here, it is not you who has made this. Or perhaps it is—your dream, your phantom other. The idea that you have somehow brought this on yourself is unbearable. You bury the music box under the bedclothes where it will not be seen and you bury your shame there too and concentrate on the sluggishness of your own blood, dragging through your veins.

Dad comes in and sits on your bed, his broad hand smoothing the hair back from your forehead, and tells you gently that Charlie passed away during the night. You are astonished that you need to be told, because of course you already know, the knowledge thuds at the heart of you.

"Come downstairs and have some breakfast," Dad says. "You've slept and slept."

You pull on track pants and a T-shirt and pad downstairs. To the left of the stairs is the family room, where the piano is now silent, but you can feel Pia is still there, her wretchedness seeps from the room, infiltrating every corner of the house and you shrink from it, but you are drawn to it too, to the power of her sorrow. Dad steers you to the right, into the kitchen.

"Pia's staying for a while," Mum tells you as she butters your toast. "With everything that happened last night there was a little scare with the pregnancy. It's all fine now—" The word *fine* resounds untruthfully in the air. Mum cuts your toast in three soldiers. "We have to be brave, Claire. We have to be strong for Pia. We can't come apart at the seams."

Pia. You stand just inside the kitchen door and listen to her silence grow. This is no longer your house, it is Despair's house. And yet the arrangement of objects in the kitchen—cups, plates and bowls laid out in their sets, the ancient, fat brown teapot in the middle of the table next to uniform triangles of toast stacked in the toast rack—is the same as any other morning, and this gives you just enough courage to sit down at the table.

The doorbell rings. Mum and Dad exchange a glance. Dad shuffles out of the kitchen to answer it. It is Mrs. Jarvis. You can't hear what they are saying, only the rise and fall of voices at the door. Dad brings her back with him into the kitchen.

"I am so sorry to intrude," Mrs. Jarvis says fretfully. "I don't want to add to your worries."

"They had a break-in," Dad says. "Last night."

Mum glances over at you. "Why don't you go outside and play, darling? It's a lovely day. Take your skipping rope, or draw a hopscotch if you like." As if you are a freckly six with pigtails instead of thirteen, almost fourteen.

But you don't argue. Your toast is the texture of cardboard. You've grown weary of chewing.

And outside it is a lovely day, it really is. The sun blooms in a cornflower sky, the houses in the street bounce red at each other. You perch on the edge of the garden wall.

You say to yourself, *Charlie is dead,* but only in your head. The words drop like gray stones. You don't *feel* anything. You think you should cry, but you can't. You think you should see how blue the sky is and be grateful for it in the face of things, but it might as well be gray, or white, or stale, sickly yellow. Nothing matters. Nothing sticks.

You feel the dog's wildness before you see it, a slinking presence on the edge of things. You feel it in the pricking of that vulnerable patch of skin on the back of your neck, you feel it pounding in your rib cage, singing in your bloodstream. You peer over your shoulder. The dog sits upright, ears erect, watching you.

You pretend to ignore it, kicking at the dirt. But the back of your neck stays up in prickles. The dog murmurs a low rumbling growl, and your heart hammers.

But the dog isn't growling at you. In the Jarvises' backyard, just in your line of sight, a woman, heavy and overdressed, with an old-fashioned hat perched on the top of her head, wide brim pressed down over her eyes, beetles from the large plum tree to another hiding spot behind the house. You almost forget the dog then.

You stand and edge over to the median strip, peering down the long wooden fence line that separates the two backyards. You can hear the murmur of adult voices in your own kitchen—Mum, Dad, Mrs. Jarvis. Not Pia, of course not Pia, whose silence billows in black cloud, drifting out of the windows and rising on the cool, crisp air, hanging over the house like a thundercloud.

The piano begins again, now playing the music-box song (it was always Charlie's favorite), and into the black clouds leaks a liquid silver, strange and familiar. The dog barks twice. You look down and at your feet there is a curling scrap of torn paper, trapped in the thick stems of a clump of native grass. The paper flutters indecisively between the two houses. You bend over and retrieve it. On one side it says in careful crouching print: *antibiotics*. On the other is written this:

IOU
a reciprocal kindness
to be redeemed by the bearer
when need arises
according to their own purpose

The dog barks again, echoing distantly in your ears, distorting into a heavy metallic sound. When you look up your house is all but gone, though the fog of Pia's sadness remains, clinging darkly to the newly white sky.

Claire stares at the place where her house used to be. The brick is crumbling to rubble, the color leaching out of it, from red to brown, now orange, or is it scorched gray, or is there no color left in the world to call it by? The flowers are gone. There is vegetation, but it is rank and slimy, thick growth gone wild, as though it never rained but instead a stinking mud sometimes slithered from the sky. It is the wrong shade to be called green.

The dog crosses the territory that used to be called road and slinks to Claire's side. It nudges her, and she forgets to be afraid. In fact, she is calmed by the solid fact of the dog's head under her hand: the oily bristles of its hairs, the flatness of its skull.

The fence is gone now, and so is the plum tree. The absence of everything is not sharp or wounding. They have not simply vanished, they have become implausible. Claire no longer believes in plum trees or fences.

There is an eye, a mess of gray, wiry hair, and a ridiculous hat peering round the corner of the wreck which was once the Jarvises' house.

"Excuse me," Claire says.

The eye disappears.

Claire waits. It seems she has endless patience. The eye returns.

"Go away, go away!" the owner of the eye shrieks. "You're trouble, you are, Clara girl, you'll bring *Her* all over again and then I'll be trussed up and tied. Besides, this aint your place no more. *I'm* here now. Possession and all that. But, oh, wait." Her voice changes, and she croons softly to herself. "Now, wait a minute, Dolores. Look close at what you're seeing. Look at the spectacle. Isn't it interesting?"

Dolores steps out, smoothing her hair, readjusting her hat. Her face is in a terrible condition, bruised and bloody, but she retains a certain dignity.

"Very pleased to meet you, I'm sure. This is a turn up, this is. Door never swung both ways before, not as far as I've been knowing. We can go to you, but once, mebbe twice, only when we're small enough to slip through, and only when the gap is close. Aint never known a dreamer to dream herself in. And why would you indeed? Why would you?" The woman's lips twitch with merriment at Claire's expense.

"But I saw you," Claire says. "In my place. Just now."

Dolores taps her swollen eye with a pudged-up finger. "You see, you saw, doesn't mean I was there. You peeked through the gap, that's all. You peeked through, then stepped through, and that's how it works."

"So I'm the dreamer? And you're the dream?"

Dolores stares haughtily and Claire sees that underneath that nest of hair, inside that swollen mess of contusion and gore, it is Young Mrs. Jarvis's exact eye staring out. "There's no one in this great gray city we call Sedge who wants to be called a dream." *Sedge.* It sounds to Claire like half a name; a broken name for a broken place. "We're real enough." Dolores goes on. "Realer than you are, I'll be bound."

Claire can't argue with that. Claire is of fence and plum tree, from the shadow world. This world, made of broken things and dust, is as real as anything she's ever seen. The dog—Claire looks down at the dog—is real too. The realest thing. Itself and the shadow of itself, like Pia's sadness, which continues to bleed blackly into the sky. Claire is only shadow.

"Feller belongs to both places," Dolores says, nodding at the dog. "That's true of all strays, aint it, feller? Dogs only get *fixed,*" she says, leering, "one place or the other, once they're owned. You, now..." She eyes Claire all over, like she's considering a purchase. Claire wants to crawl out from under her gaze, but where would she go? "You on the other hand is a singular specimen. I wonder now, if it's the swapping of them jingle-jangles what's brought you through."

"Jingle-jangles?" Claire blinks. Dolores seems to dwell only just inside language, she makes sentences the way a potter works clay, squashing them any which way into shapes that please her. A liquid tiredness threatens to overwhelm Claire as she works to understand. "Oh. You mean the music boxes? *My* music box?"

"Yours, yes, as much as one thing can own another, as much as a thing wants to be owned. And the other. Broken it were, and terrible cracked, but along came a girl who saw something in it, like I knew she would. And so she signed her name and bought it. Carried her some of the way, that broken box, and what did she find on the other side but the same one only plump with wholeness, all lovely, and didn't that girl want it? So you ended up with the first one, the sorry broken mess. And your precious one *she* took. But she left it to rot up there, in the damp and the dark, where her guilt wouldn't be arrested by the sight of it."

Claire curls the paper in her hand. She looks up at the rubble where Dolores is pointing, where her house once was. *Her* music box, taken and lost, abandoned. So close up there, but beyond her reach . . .

Claire thinks of Clara and feels rage at her, fury at what she has taken: Claire's living memory of Charlie, and with it her ability to grieve. For that must be why this numbness has clasped her heart, this blankness in the face of Charlie's death.

"What's this? What do we have here? Let me look, let me feast my eyes. . . ." Dolores snatches the paper from Claire's hand before Claire finds the wits to hold it away from her or hide it. The old woman reads it greedily. " 'Reciprocal kindness'?" she laughs. Then: " 'Redeemed by the bearer'?" she muses. " 'According to their own purpose'? Hum."

She moves to poke it down her cleavage, collector of names that she is, but Claire snatches it back.

Dolores pins her good eye on Claire. "You fixing to save that wicked child? She's beyond saving, that one, that one what stole from you the very piece of your heart. Why should you pity her when she has shown no pity to you?"

Claire stares at Dolores. Why would she pity Clara?

Trespasser, enemy, thief. Clara, who is now the safe one, kept from harm, kept from grief, with every meal provided for. Claire can still taste the dream of sweet on the tip of her tongue. Why should Claire feel for Clara when Clara felt nothing for Claire—not pity, not even scorn. Nothing.

"You got to wonder, don't you, girl?" Dolores sings out as Claire turns away, even as the place around her dissolves into colors and the dreamworld, Sedge, drains away. Piano notes fall one by one from the white sky, clattering to the world below like tin forks and spoons. "Who owes who owes who? Seems to me now Clara owes you."

"I'm going to the shops," Mum says, standing at the front door, jangling her keys. "Want to come?"

You do, but you don't. You consider the alternatives.

"I'll be leaving in five minutes," she says.

You move yourself up the stairs to your room. The music box is an unsightly bulge under the bedcovers. What if Dad finds it? What if Pia does? What would they think? That you broke it on purpose? You stuff it into a backpack, shrug the bag on, and slink downstairs to find your mother.

"Where's Pia?" you ask.

"Sleeping, finally. The doctor gave her something to help her rest, something that won't hurt the baby."

You wonder what black dreams scribble themselves around Pia's head.

"What's in the bag?" Mum asks.

You look at her. You almost don't answer but then you say, "Charlie's music box."

"Oh, sweetie," she says. Her eyes brim, but you cannot feel anything for yourself or for her.

As the car glides down the main road, you catch glimpses up the side streets of the wild green growth along the riverbanks.

Your mum looks at the backpack on your lap. "You know, what I said about being brave for Pia. I shouldn't have said that. It's okay to grieve Charlie. It's okay to cry if you want."

You hear a catch in her throat. You look sideways at your mother and see her eyes are leaking. It's not that you don't want to. But you can't cry. You just can't.

"Charlie knew that we loved him," Mum says. "We have that."

In the supermarket car park you hang back. Mum leads the way, but you don't exactly follow, making your own path through the hatchbacks and sedans and four-wheel-drives, lined up like sentries, with their dulled yet watchful eyes. There is a roaring in your ears so as to deafen you, and you can no longer hear Mum hurrying you along. The straps of your backpack dig into your shoulders. You catch a glimpse of dog between the cars and you whistle softly. The whistle seems to unstick the air that sways gray and steely over the rows and rows of parked cars and they ripple, as if they are not present at all, merely projections of color and light.

You whistle again, and then, without meaning to, you

hum. You tra-la-la. You sing the notes of the music box, and it seems to you that the box trembles ever so slightly inside the bag on your back, as though it is recognizing the song of itself. You are not even sure if it is you that is making the song or if the song is passing through you, using you as its instrument.

The world alters, with shudders and creaks. You feel your own place peel away to reveal Sedge, which was there all along. You are awake and you are dreaming again.

The market is hum and jostle, bustle and quarrel, thick with folk.

Claire cannot take it in all at once, she has to elbow her way through the crowds, catching snatches of sights between. It calls itself a market, but it is more like a rubbish tip, with broken and half-used-up things spread around, and all the people selling and buying look broken or used up themselves. Claire can sketch in her mind the car park, minus the cars, and not so cleanly made as the place she just stepped from. Claire feels suddenly conspicuous, with her clean fingernails and tidy clothes and combed hair.

Claire is vaguely aware of a distant rumbling, a familiar noise, like a plane passing high in the sky. It doesn't seem alarming, but people go from staring at her to glancing uncomfortably toward the sky. Is there a quickening in the air, an undercurrent of unease brewing?

"Here," says one old hag, catching Claire by surprise, long yellow fingers grasping Claire's hair sharply and pulling at the roots. "Look at you, Clara, all cleaned up. I heard you been kept by Our Lady and now I see with my own eyes, large as life, dolly and priss."

"Hush up, Trinka," says another, older than the first and mucky too, but not so hook-nosed. "Leave her be." The first old filth, Trinka, drops Claire's hair. The second scowls Trinka away, then says to Claire with a pat of the ground: "You come here to Mudda Meggsy and wile and tattle the time, like we always done." Her words are friendly, if her countenance isn't, and Claire cannot find her tongue to say no.

Claire steps over the thread-worn blanket and half cakes of soap covered in grime and sits beside Mudda Meggsy. Mudda Meggsy lowers her voice. "I don't know what you're thinking, but you should not be coming here."

Claire peers around for the dog. Mudda Meggsy has obviously mistaken her for Clara, thinking she's skedaddled from Boedica.

"You aint Clara," Mudda Meggsy says, smiling her unlovely smile at passing customers. "I got two eyes. You be getting back where you from, quicksmart. Or you get lost here, and that aint good for no one, not for you, nor Clara, nor the balancing up of this and that. When things tip, they slide."

That rumble passes through the air again, but this time it's closer, like the plane has dropped altitude.

"What do I care what happens to Clara? She stole something of mine. She made the world unstuck."

"Works the same both ways. You can't come here 'cept by the very deepness of your wanting. You *wanted* yourself here, sure as mud. And you can want yourself back again, quicksmart."

Claire isn't sure that wanting is something she can control. It's like appetite. The only way to control it is to feed it. And she can't have the only thing she really wants, Charlie alive again. Though, she muses, if she can't have that, she wants her music box back. Is that the desire that's brought her here? But she knows where the box is, doesn't she? She knows it sits an arm's reach—a world away—from her own bedroom door.

Claire walks around the market. Most of the market-goers regard her as neither here nor there, not worth glancing at twice. There are some who confuse her for Clara and make fun of her smoothed hair and tidy manner or—if they know Clara as Lady Boedica's—watch from a distance and puzzle at the Lady's new pet being let loose to wander, glancing about to see if someone has it tamed.

But still there are others who, like Mudda Meggsy, recognize Claire. A surprising number of them, she notices, who recoil with disgust and fear, or frown with anger at her carelessness, as if it is where she hails from that is the bad place and Sedge that is all innocence and safety. Whenever one of the rumbles come—so loud now they seem to clatter the teeth—it is Claire these ones look to, as though she is dragging that rumbling in her wake, though she has no idea what it could be.

Finally Claire spies the dirty matted rump of the dog

ahead. Finding a gap in the crowds, she shoves her way toward it. But again it slithers away.

There are the two sisters—sweet and sour—clutching each other as they basket their wares, selling and swapping the stitchings they've made. They see Claire and their faces diverge. The pretty one thinks, clear as day, You are Clara escaped. She smiles widely, as if her lips can't help but stretch, though Claire can see she is furious beneath. The other *recognizes,* sees right through Claire's skin, and she frowns, but is more curious than anything else.

"Clara!" says Aily.

"That's never Clara," Greya assures. "Didn't you leave her with Fat Aitch not an hour before this one? As if he would ever let her slipper away. No, this is"—she eyes Claire, as if to read her identity in her face—*"someone else."*

"Claire," Claire says, for isn't that her name? Isn't it? She finds she can only just capture the shape of it. It seems all of a sudden unfinished, ending in *air.*

Aily's smile widens, all spleen. "You must be sisters, then," she says, "for you are alike as eggs, though not so differently named as sisters mostly are."

"Here," says Greya, pushing her basket into Aily's hands. "You do the offering and milktongue, you're always better at it than I."

Aily smiles and smiles, her eyebrows raised, staring her sister down, then takes the basket and walks a little ahead, fluttering and flirting with women and men, old and young, but her eyes flicker constantly to check Greya is close.

"You should not be here," Greya hisses.

"I didn't choose to come. The dog brought me," Claire protests, but she thinks of Mudda Meggsy, who said she had wished herself here. "At least, I think it was the dog."

"A dog, is it?" says Greya. "A stray? That'd be right. This smells ripe of dog."

"Clara left this behind. In my . . . place." Claire tugs the backpack off and opens it, showing Greya the hated box. "And instead she took mine and I want it. I want it back."

Greya groans and pushes the backpack away. "Put it away, you galumph. I wish I'd never seen it. I aint getting involved, this is nothing to me. I can see the wrongness of you, it makes me sick to look at you, like a broken leg all twisted the wrong way."

"Well, I can't help it! I need the dog to get me home, and even then I don't know if it's the dog alone that makes it work."

The ground groans and shudders. Marketeers gather their goods closer and customers hurry to finish their transactions.

Aily marches over. "We gotta go back. You got watching work to do this night." She takes Greya's arm jealously.

"In a minute," says Greya, shrugging her lightly away. "We're all but finished here, my Aily. Go on. Find a one more wants buying, or ten."

Aily stalks off, sunshine and light on her face, a storm brewing beneath.

Greya turns on Claire. "You find that dog, you get yourself back. You buy that dog a meatstick and a collar and give that dog a name to call it by. Own that dog and make it stay."

"I'm not going," Claire says. She crosses her arms. "Not until I get my music box back."

"Course you're going. There aint no way in life you can stop here. It'll pull you all to pieces." Greya laughs suddenly, still scowling. "You look just like your other one, all chin."

"She's not me. I'm not her. She is nothing to me."

"You cannot put yourself to rights without her," Greya muses. "But don't be thinking to rescue her, Lady would only add you to her set."

"Why would I do that?" Claire snaps. "She's just a thing I've dreamed, and so are you, so is it all! Sedge is a dream, it was invented in my head, and grew from me, every bit of it." She wants to wound Greya, but Greya shrugs. Despite Dolores's warning, she doesn't seem to care about being called a dream.

"Then it is you what dreamed your music box broke."

And then, bouncing off the tops of the heads of the marketeers, a name echoes, originating from here, the marketplace, but echoing all around the great city of Sedge: *Claire! Claire!* A name all would hear: Boedica, Dolores and her mother, Groom, the cowardly Ketch. Even Clara, distant, indifferent Clara, princess of the keep, would hear it, bouncing around the sheltering stone walls.

Each call is a terrible cymbal crash in the sky and the whole market flinches at the unearthly sound. The name is strange even to Claire's own ear, it sounds unfinished in this place. She doesn't want to own it yet, but she knows it is trying to claim her. Metal ghosts with headlight eyes flicker briefly into space and then vanish.

Greya holds Claire's eyes, despite the rush of wind around them, despite the fact that the world is caving in. "I don't think you wanted yourself here for the music box at all," Greya accuses her. "I think this is what you wanted."

"I don't know what you mean."

"A broken world for a broken girl."

Aily comes back and presses her fingernails into Greya's arm, grinning with fear. "Come *on,* sister."

Claire grabs Greya's other arm, trying to hold herself in Sedge, and Aily tugs back, wrenching Greya free. The sisters are lost in the quickening crowd, but not so hopelessly lost as Claire.

Claire can feel the pull Greya spoke of (she's felt it all along), only now it's a huge physical yank, like the market-place is contracting around her to propel her out. She goes down on all fours, because it hurts, and because Greya is right, she is broken.

The dog comes snuffling around her, whines and lays down with its head between its paws. She grabs it by the scruff, to leave, but also for comfort, and with one echoing baritone bark, Sedge snaps away in a rush of wind and cacophony.

The place settles to rights around you, the car park, the cars, the supermarket, the pearly blue winter sky, the cold seeping out of the ground, and high above a flock of black birds making shapes out of themselves. Kneeling between parked cars, you bury your face in the dog, which smells of Sedge. The music box is lost, and Charlie is lost, and you are lost.

But the dog is real against you, and you feel something for the dog. You *want* it, is what you feel. You want to have it and keep it. You want it to be your dog, and you want it to own you back.

You hear your mother calling desperately, "Claire Claire Claire!"

You call back, "I'm here!" because the sound of her voice cracking apart with terror is unbearable. She calls again, you call back, and she follows the sound of your voice to find you.

"For God's sake, I've been calling and calling, why didn't you answer me before?"

"I've found a dog."

"Well, don't touch it, you don't know where it's been."

"I want it."

"Claire, somebody must own it."

"No, they don't. It's a stray. Look, no collar."

"Then we'll call the pound."

"They'll lock it up! They'll put it down! Please, can't we take it home?"

"Claire. When things have settled, when everything's over and done with . . ."

"Settled?" you ask, without expression. You are curious to know. "When will it be settled? When will it be done with?"

"Claire, you're asking too much. This isn't the right time . . . this isn't the day for—"

"This *is* the time. This is the only time. This is the right dog."

Mum sighs. "That creature is not getting into our car. We'll never get rid of the smell."

"Fine. I'll walk home."

Mum hugs herself and, surprising you, she nods. You think she looks small and far away.

"I'll get a tin of dog food," Mum says.

"And a collar? And its own bowl?"

"Don't push your luck, Claire. I haven't said we can keep it."

"I know." But you allow yourself a small victorious smile, just the same.

You walk home through the forgiving pale light of the winter afternoon, taking your time about it, because it is the first time you have walked a dog, and you only wish you had waited for Mum to buy a collar and a lead, because you are nervous that at any point it will take off, toward the river, or slip through a dog-sized loopway into Sedge and be lost.

You lock the dog in the backyard and watch it run twitching from shrub to tree to fence post, feasting on the smells. It lies down on the grass, rolls over, rubs the smell of your place onto itself. It comes to you and you wrap your arms around it and whisper into its neck.

"Sandy? Jim? A plain name, you aren't a fancy dog. But you have a little music in you, so not too plain. Not Rover. No, not Jim. It has to be perfect."

You know Mum will not have it in the house, but you sneak it inside to find Dad and show him your dog. He is sitting on the piano stool and Pia on the couch. You want to nestle beside her, under the crook of her arm, and press your head to her belly to listen to the rippling waterdance of the baby. But you see Dad has the phone in his hands, and Pia is fingering through an address book. She closes her eyes for a minute.

"Do you want a break?" Dad asks.

Pia shakes her head. She puts her finger on another number and passes it to Dad, who makes the call. To tell everyone the world has been remade. Broken and put together again, but put together badly, because there is no Charlie in it.

You back out of the room before the person on the other end can answer. Before they can all agree to call this a world, regardless, before life begins the dull machinery of getting on with things, after the event, after Charlie, ex post facto.

The dog balks at the bottom of the stairs, sitting on its rump. Softly you cajole, beg, entreat, wishing you had a name to call it by. Eventually you give it a gentle shove from behind and up it goes, following the residual scent trail of its own pungency, into your bedroom. You take out the broken music box and hold it, and once again you hum that creaking tune.

The dog paces wildly in your room, knocking things from the shelf with its great, worried, beating tail. It whimpers. You keep humming, staring at the door, behind—or *within*—which is another door, a door that leads back to Sedge.

You can't help the longing that assails you, for the music box that was yours. For Charlie. Oh, you know Charlie is gone. You know nothing will restore him. But you want to hold on tight to the idea of Charlie, you want to conjure him every night in your dreams.

You thought you knew the rules of passage from this world to the next. You thought you had it all worked out: the dog, the music box, the tune. You thought you could bend Sedge to your will too, but you can't. You can't.

Try as you might, you cannot make your own dreams.

Suddenly the dog growls at you, showing the whites of its eyes, curling a lip to bare a broken tooth. You recoil, alarmed. You realize, all at once, what you have done, bringing something wild, something untamed into your room, something with viciousness in its heart as well as faithfulness. And who is it faithful to?

The dog barks, and the sound, rich and guttural, threatens to tear apart the quiet house. You edge past the dog and open your bedroom door. It follows you back downstairs. You cannot help thinking of those yellow teeth snapping at your ankles, but the dog is docile and obedient, as if the growl never happened. When it gets outside it breaks into a hopeful, lopsided gallop, caught short by the borders of the fence. Quivering, it sniffs the boundaries of the garden and you watch it go round and round, trampling plants, threading its way through the winter-flowering creeper with its tremulous purple flowers.

Finally it lays itself down at the back gate, its nose wedged into the gap underneath, its body still quivering, as if it is inhaling the tantalizing scents of delicious, sweet freedom, and suddenly, with sharp, almost unbearable remorse you think of Clara, the stale air *she* breathes, trapped in the stony chambers of Boedica's wanting heart.

Remember. The music box always had an eccentric habit: a slight change in the atmosphere, or perhaps the faintest breath of wind, a sharp step in the hall outside, or even the breeze of a mouse brushing past the bookshelf . . . and a surge of music would pour out, as if it had been wound anew.

Sometimes, when you were little and you couldn't sleep,

your mother would lie beside you on hot summer nights and together you would listen to the music box and feel haunted by it, the eerie music tumbling across the room and along the hallway in the dark, quiet house. She would tell you of that moment in the hospital bed, holding you, her baby girl, for the very first time, gazing down at you with a fierce, devotional hunger, and how her little brother, Charlie, your uncle—Charlie, who could charm his way past any midwife or obstetrician, despite the fact that you hadn't even left the labor room yet—burst into the room, breathing heavily, shocked into silence at the sight of you, the music box tucked under his arm suddenly coming to life, to everyone's surprise but yours, for in this world everything was new, all color and light and agitation, and what use had you yet for astonishment?

Night is fallen. Sedge is far away. But as you fall toward sleep, a burst of music lifts you from yourself. You are Claire and you are not Claire, a pale ghost of yourself, adrift. You look down and see the empty body you have left behind, weighted to the bed. This is the music of Charlie, carrying you, bearing you upward. It is almost as though you are carried by Charlie, he is holding on to the very lightness of you.

You drift through the rooms of your own house, over the bodies of your sleeping parents, the shape of them, each alone in their dreaming, but entwined on the island of their shared bed, as if carrying each other.

You are propelled over the darkness of Pia. She sprawls

on the bed, her nightie stretched tight over her belly, her leg on a pillow, her arm stretched out into empty space. The music wants you to linger here, to watch her sleep, but it is too intimate. You urge yourself onward, dreaming yourself outside, pushing against the music's tidal surge.

The dog is asleep and dreaming too, whimpering and twitching. You rise up, over the house and look down on the roof that holds them all in, those dreamers.

And you see Sedge and your own place hastily pinned together, one on top of the other, like a skirt waiting to be sewn, raw unfinished ends and loose threads, turned inside out to reveal only the drab underside of the vivid print.

You long for the music box—your very own thing—and with a ghost's long-wanting arms you reach down toward it, but there is too much momentum, you are whisked and whirled, swept, eddied. You see broken buildings, teeming with wild cats and Raiders and dogs in the streets, and you swear you see Dolores, beetling under her hat from one shadow to the next. You drift over Doctor's and see Ketch on the doorstep, mucking out a bucket of black slime. You see the night markets, the thin curls of smoke, hear the quickening tempo of drums, and you hover, darkly curious about bursting time. But the music knows it's not for you, and hurries you along on a warm current of air.

You rise higher and from far above you see Groom, a small figure in the laneways between old factories and warehouses, waiting, his shoulders hunched over, kicking up the last dregs of hope with every dragging step. You are half in love with Groom yourself, and you want to breeze right through the flesh of him, but you can't linger, for you know where you're heading now.

It is to Boedica's palace that Charlie's music has brought you. Sedge stops flickering and becomes still and fixed, solid and stone, but you are still spirit. You pour yourself through an invisible crack in the wall as thin as the opening of an envelope, and you travel down passageways and all the time you feel, not borne now, but tugged, toward yourself and not-yourself, the girl in the dream: Clara.

Greya is keeping watch this night, and she sees *something,* some shuddering of the air. She frowns and frowns at Clara, lying sleeping on the bed, and you think she will fix Clara here with her eye. But you also think Greya may have a heart for Clara, may know what it's like to wish herself somewhere else, and that is why she recognized you at the markets. And indeed, as she bends to light a candle, she looks furtively around her. And then hurries out of the room, brushing through the swirling breath of wind that is you.

You are left alone with Clara.

There she lies sleeping, dreaming dreams of her own, and you realize she is dreaming you now, that this is what has brought you here, not in your body but out of it. And her sadness is Pia's sadness, heavy and dark, and you realize with a shock of recognition that it is *your* sadness, this is your face you are seeing, your loss, your grief. And you want to wake her, you long to, but she sleeps on and you are air, the air of Claire, and you cannot make an impression on her dreams. But you know what you must do.

I can hear music. Can you hear it, Clara? Andrew whispers in my ear. It's sweet. It hurts.

I wake from my dreaming and I hear it—the glory—and yes. It does hurt. Here in the halfway place between wake and dream, my heart bursts open and grief comes rushing in.

Run, Clara, Andrew tells. Get out of this place before you fade into shadows and nothing.

I open my eyes and I am crying. Why am I crying, Andrew?

And look, there I am, flickering against the wall, like I was already turned: shadows and nothing. Only it aint me, it's *her.* That girl from the other side of dreaming, from fairyland, and it's her tears, the ones she can't make herself, that burn my face. And she opens her mouth, as if to speak, but what comes out is not words, but a billowing black cloud. And there is music all round her, silvery bright, but fading,

fading, and she is fading too, the strands of her barely coming together. Her face gets desperate with all the sounds not coming out. I lean forward to *listen*.

Once more she opens her mouth and this time I see words, silver words pouring out of her. *Run, Clara. Run, Clara. Run run run.*

I close my eyes. I am tired and sad, too tired to run. And then I am jolted to my feet by a deafening crack, lightning trapped under the earth's crust lunging upward. The girl is gone, and I am awake, blood coursing through me.

A candle flickers, casting shadows and light, but no one is there to be lit, not the ghostie girl and not the frowning one who was supposed to be watching this night. She aint in my room where she sat at day's end, and she aint in the vestibule either. She's gone, leaving only her light behind.

I hear again the memory of the crack, the sharp sound of stone separating from itself, and I go looking, huddling against the stone walls, barefooting along the corridors, hoarding that candle light behind a cupped hand, breath held ready to puff it out. The light bounces back to me and I think that crack is a dream and nothing more, and I am sure to be caught, and my heart slams against my ribs like a bird on glass.

I aint tired now. I'm awake, more awake than I've ever been, my blood ticks in my veins. If there aint no broken-apart walls then I'll get out another way, I'll climb to the roof and fly like a bird.

But here is a place where the light won't go, where brick crumbles from brick, where stone is cleaved in two, a rupture in the walls where darkness bleeds into darkness. It's a narrow crack, but it'll do me.

I hesitate. Up there somewhere, in her high rooms, Boedica watches over us all, the ones she's collected, parent and infant and child, man and woman and beast and bird, with her bright empty eyes. She tries to feed her emptiness, mistaking it for appetite, but it grows and it grows and it grows.

Now that all this feeling is opened up inside me, I almost feel something for her. But I gotta run and it aint nothing to do with what Dolores teased when she saw me, it's to do with my own wild self. I gotta keep running till I'm free to choose my own life or I will end up tatters and ghosts, that's all.

Andrew is gone. And I gotta live with the sadness and put it next to something like hope, or that sadness is for nothing, it's a tune for dying to, that's all, that's all, and Andrew wants me to live, to the fullness of my self. I want me to live to the fullness of my self.

In the darkness I hear the rolling voices of Duguld and Brown and if I stand here feeling sorry for Boedica they will find me, and aint neither of them ever spared a care for me. I work my body through that crack. It squeezes me tight and holds me and if it won't let go I'll be found here, half in, half out, straddling two places all at once.

They are coming, closer, closer and I will be caught. I am holding my breath and that is what's keeping me stuck, and when I let it out in a rush, I deflate nice and easy and then I am through.

She will hunt me down, chase me to the edge of the river,

but she won't cross it, this I know, for her territory, her whole known world, ends there.

I run on slippered feet into the shadows and freedom quickens my heart. Somewhere hiding in this black night is Groom, and he wants to be found.

You wake in your own bed. The music continues to leak between the worlds and the door of your room gleams silver. You hear the dog bark, once, twice. You leap out of bed and in the time between heartbeats you snatch up the broken music box and dive between doors.

There you are, looking at the interior of your own house, the soft spongy bones, the colorless wallpaper peeling like sheaths of dead skin, the cobwebs and dust, the desolate emptiness. If you step forward it would be into dizzying space, the sagging floor giving way beneath you. You feel hope escaping you, in this place. That is what this place does, squeezes hope out of you, out of your heart, out of the very air.

The broken house is dark, desolate, and then your eyes alight on the exact thing you seek, your music box, gleaming with its own brightness. You place the broken one at the threshold between worlds and take up your whole, perfect one. Your inside self surges with loneliness for the broken box, for the life it will have here in this gray, abandoned place. But you can't have Sedge and lose it too. You must get back to your own world with only what belongs to you. You fold up Andrew's IOU and tuck it safely under the broken music box.

With the music's last breath you cross back, into your world, into your place, into the safe arms of home.

You stand in your room holding the box in your arms. You turn the key and it plays perfectly ordinary music. You lower yourself to the floor. You close your eyes to conjure him, Charlie, and there he is, the closeness of his bristling chin, the warm spice of him, the laughter in his throat. And he is near, but he is so absent, so utterly vanished, so completely disappeared. And you let yourself feel it: the gaping hole of him, the unbearable loss, which you must bear. You must. And your sorrow overwhelms you, and you are rasping great ugly breaths and your mother comes in and finds you there, and she kneels beside you and holds you, and rocks you back and forward as you cry and cry and—

In the morning the dog is gone.

Your parents come outside to help you search for it. Though none of you can find a point of exit (the gate is firmly shut), the dog has somehow vamoosed the yard. Tears spring into your eyes as you call for it—*Dog! Dog!*—for you have no name to call it by.

"A mystery," says Dad.

"I swear it wasn't me," says Mum. "I might even have taken to it. It had a nice face."

"It'll be back," says Dad. "When it gets hungry."

You shake your head. It won't be back. It was halfway owned after all, just not by you.

"Ah, well," says Dad, and rubs you on the shoulder. You bury your face into his chest. He puts his arm around you.

Your mother starts walking the fence line again, looking for evidence of the mysteriously disappeared dog.

"Maybe we could get a puppy," you say.

"*May*-be," says Mum, not making any promises. "Or an adult dog from the pound. One that's already house-trained."

"A stray?" You consider this. "Maybe. If it chooses us."

Pia sits in the living room. She sees you standing in the doorway, the music box in your arm.

"Darling Claire."

You sit beside her and nuzzle in. You press your cheek to the babe who swims under her skin. Your salt water soaks through Pia's dress, leaving unsightly splotches.

"We lost him, the three of us. It was stupid of us to lose him. Wasn't it, Pia?"

Pia curls a lock of your hair on her finger. "He is close," Pia says.

You put the music box on the coffee table in front of her.

"For the baby."

"Oh, Claire. You don't have to—"

"I *want* to."

She hugs you close to her side.

The baby pirouettes in the dappled dark, singing itself into being.

And this is where I leave you, Claire, the dreamer, half listening (as you always will now) for the ache of music pressing on the other side of the air, rising from a mostly forgotten dream. I am a dreamer too, and I must wake into a world of dreamers. You can feel it—can't you?—the peeling off of me, another small loss you have to bear. We all bear it, as best we can, this infinite chain of miniature losses, a hundred thousand stories, a hundred thousand endings. A rehearsal, you could call it, for the last ending that's bound to come, eventually, somewhere in the white space between here and dreaming.

The dog pads through market, following a rich trail of smells. This scent map leads it all round the city, head and tail.

"Told you that dog'd be back, didn't I tell you that, Mother?"

"Local galloper. Scored a tough win. Makes her own luck."

From market it follows the scent to Doctor's, where it's kicked for its troubles. The kicker is Ketch, who never said he were brave. The dog scares him something dreadful with its knowing eyes, and who knows what it might whiff on Ketch. Even after being kicked, the dog takes a long hard sniff and smells Andrew being buried in black clay, but not afore Doctor tells a last goodbye, to his favorite, to his best boy.

At Boedica's walled town the dog stops and inhales the

color out of the world: all them smells weaving into its head, mapping sadness and despair till its heart is black from emptiness. It sniffs hopelessness, and it almost gives up, lies down to be found by Boedica's troops, and you know who they're hunting, don't you? Though she aint made that call yet. Soon. Not yet. The dog sniffs the sharp wits of the girl with the orange hair and is pleased with her, for she will always get by.

At the last, it sniffs a tasty dish, better to a dog than liver and bacon, it sniffs out hope it does, it sniffs out freedom. And it follows that sniff down to the river, sniffing up love and courage and companionship, through the gloom of the evergreen, through the rushes and the weeds.

Through the organic growth it's coming. It's coming to find us where we lie sleeping, and it will join us by and by. For there's only ever always a long journey to go.

"I had a dream," Groom tells. "It was you and me. We was travelin to make somethin new. A beginnin." He lays his hand on mine, and I twitch with the warmth of it. "Let's make a beginnin, Clara?"

I keep my hand in his. "This day?"

"Some day. Some night or other."

We stand at river's edge, watching the brown water swirl.

"This night," I say. The undergrowth stirs behind me, and there she is. My dog, who found us when we were crouched up sleeping, just as I dreamed a name to call her by.

"Charley." I beckon her. She comes to the water's edge and

whimpers. One of my hands rests on her brindled neck. The other stays folded in Groom's. "Charley," I whisper. "It's time to go."

Groom hesitates. He tightens his grip. "What do you think we'll find on the other side?"

"Us," I say. "You and me." And I walk in to the cool rushing river, still holding Groom's hand.

AUTHOR'S NOTE

Whatever you think about Freud, he was clearly on to something when he said that a great internal drama plays out in kids between the ages of three and five. When I began sketching Clara together with words, I had half an eye on my eldest daughter, Fred. The motif of doubles in the novel came about after a conversation we had when she was four and we were listening to our heartbeats.

Fred: What does it mean?
Me: It means my heart is busy pumping blood all over my body. It means I'm alive and so are you.
Fred: What happens when you get this people again?
Me: Which people?
Fred: This people (she points to herself).
Me: Another person just like you?
Fred: Yes.
Me: That never happens. You are unique. There is only one little girl like you in the whole wide world. Just one Frederique.
Fred: (sadly) Oh, pleeease.

I too had lain in bed as a child, trying to picture the whole world's population. The world was so inconceivably big to me as to seem infinite, and if it was infinite, I was sure that meant there had to be another girl, just like me—no, not *just like,* but me, another me—living a parallel life somewhere on the other side of the world. I envisaged the world not so much as a ball, but as a coin, with two almost identical halves. The idea that I could be alone in the universe, that I was unique, was unbearably sad.

In the period of my life that Fred and I had this conversation I was writing a thesis at Melbourne University as part of a masters in creative writing, entitled *Melancholy Ever After,* about the effect of melancholy on narrative structure in fairy tales. This novel is an indirect response to the ideas I was chasing in that thesis, and the problems I uncovered in fairy tales where children remained in their fairy-tale landscapes, forever locked into their childhood bodies—Peter Pan is really very creepy.

I would like to take this opportunity to acknowledge and thank my fellow students and the academic staff, in particular Kevin Brophy, who supervised this thesis and helped me find my voice as an academic. Also visiting tutors Olga Lorenzo, Rod Jones, Claire Gaskin and especially Carrie Tiffany, whose writing exercise gave Old Mrs. Jarvis her horse-racing obsession, and her words.

Sometimes I think if I sit very still, and listen very carefully, my children might reveal something true about the universe. This happens more often than you might think, at least three times a day. Frederique and Una are both in this novel: the parts of myself that are shaped by them, the tangle of their thoughts, the atmosphere they create in the house when it is night and they are sleeping. Even Avery, who was born at the end of the writing process, dreamed himself into the story.

Lili Wilkinson, Slimejam (Christopher Miles), Cochineal (Rachel Holkner) and Sushipyjamas (Kate Whitfield) read and gave feedback on drafts, and also got me out of the house after dark. Kate Constable also read drafts, but I mostly have to thank her for loving Clara and understanding Claire. To Kirsty Murray, who has been organizing me into things for over ten years, thank you so much. I always listen to everything you say. You have very authoritative hair.

The phrase "only ever always" sprang from the space that lies between my friend Zoë and me, a space that stretches and shifts but never grows apart. We have known each other so long, I am not sure whose memories are whose anymore.

Emily shared Rupert Brooke with me and I thank her for it with fond affection. We were fifteen and she was madly in love with him, even though he'd been dead for seventy-five years.

Finally, spending a day scouring and sifting and quarrying the debris of your imagination is a strange and sometimes lonely job. Martin keeps a light on, and guides me home.

ABOUT THE AUTHOR

Penni Russon was born in Hobart, Australia, and spent her childhood roaming around on a small mountain. Eventually she had to grow up, and she moved from Tasmania to Melbourne to study classics, archaeology, women's studies and contemporary literature. She writes, edits, and teaches creative writing, and lives in outer Melbourne with her husband and three children.

Find out more about Penni at pennirusson.com or on her blog, eglantinescake.blogspot.com.